How Delightful Is the Day

A novel by **Gabe Oppenheim**

Solicitude, Inc.   New York

For Mom, Dad and Jon.
And for Grandpa.

An Introduction to the Collegiate Journal of Jeremiah Goldstein

In light of what happened to Jeremiah, the decision to publish his journal was an easy one. He was always writing, and always hoping to have his stuff read, and while I'm reasonably certain he never intended to publish it, he surely meant to use the material later, in other works.

I knew about the journal because one night, in the period of freshman year during which we shared an apartment, he mentioned it in passing. I had said something about how hard it is to recall poignant episodes we experience for later use in writing. He then mumbled something about daily journal entries. It was as though he wanted to tell me but also to keep it secret. I asked whether he in fact kept such a journal, and, without a word, he nodded. I had been standing on the threshold of his room, and at that moment, I began to step in.

But he swiveled his desk chair back toward the computer, signaling an end to the conversation, and I was rebuffed.

Only later, months later, maybe even the night before I flew back to Atlanta for the summer, did I finally see a page (though I had seen him write an entry once on a train, not knowing at the time what he was up to). I hadn't started packing yet, not really, and he was sitting there, as usual, over his desk, pecking away at the flimsy plastic keys of the shit laptop we each owned. "Can I see a page now?" I asked.

And the way he silently bent over, pulled out a drawer and removed a single sheaf from a hefty stack, led me to believe he understood: that it was summer now, and friends apart tended to drift, and this sort of shared intimacy would firm our bond for the long months of separation.

We were warm, tight buddies, back then.

We would drift in the next three years, first as Jeremiah sunk into himself and then later as he poured everything into his work and new girlfriend. I did not quite comprehend it – the way he could spend all his time conceiving and writing and just plain dreaming, and I'm not saying I get it now in light of what happened. Because, let's be honest – even though Jeremiah was deathly afraid of dying, even though he spent sophomore year under the firm belief that if he didn't complete a book now he never would because he would soon be dead and even though Jeremiah often worried about waking up one day, inexplicably, without any of the talent he previously possessed, those beliefs were nonsense – so much so that, by the time Jeremiah was sleeping normally at night senior year, he himself had dismissed them all. Except the one about losing talent.

Talent, actually, was the root of the tension between us – which made things uncomfortable when we first met and increasingly hostile with each new development. Basically, I could tell, almost from the first week of school – for he was by then competing with me for a columnist position with the school newspaper – that his ambition and naturalness would go unmatched. And because of that, whenever he faltered – and he did, occasionally, especially when he went sleepless and mad like a zombie – I made sure to let him know, rub it in – as if hoping to make permanent the temporary shift in our fortunes. Of course, one cannot do that. A single good night's sleep rearranged everything again. I had my own writing position, with the campus alternative weekly. You can understand how I felt.

I say all this now, honestly, because it doesn't matter. It's too late to matter, and, even if it weren't, I still might be comfortable admitting the obvious. The truth is, I was never cut out to write like he wrote, just as none of us can quite duplicate the other. He had his talents, which lent themselves to deep, layered stories, and I had mine, which lent themselves more to rhetorical flourish and ornamentation. Even a bit of humor, if I may. I was doing myself a disservice, then, by attempting to do what he did – because I could have thrived all the more if I had just stuck to my own game. Which leads me to the work set and organized before you.

The words, clearly, are Jeremiah's. This is his journal. But I've arranged it the way I have – that is, retaining some entries and omitting others – because I think the story can be better drawn out that way. In part, this is my attempt – by default, the only I'll ever have – to partner with Jeremiah and combine our talents the way we should have from the beginning. It's a musical with the lyrics by him and the music by me.[1] And I'm very grateful to the Goldstein family for letting me execute this project and in particular for allowing me to assemble his journal in the novelistic way I desired.

I do believe that in his death, my own greatest work shall emerge. He had to give way for my own abilities to unfold – for me to gain the prerequisite confidence, and material. But consider me not bold, and please do not mistake: Were I given the choice, even in my darkest moments, I'd have to keep him living and my own work in check. I could not honestly argue the world deserves the latter more than the former or that I'd benefit it more than he. This is the collegiate journal of Jeremiah Goldstein, not Mo Gross, and so it shall remain.

This publication, then, will always be bittersweet.

---

[1] Also, the footnotes are by me.

Freshman Year

Aug. 28, 2005

The things we carried from Best Buy and Bed Bath & Beyond and Pathmark:

One refrigerator, four feet tall; one laptop computer, with a free laser printer and three-year warranty; one plastic trash can with scooped out handles; one hamper made out of a giant spring and netting, which compresses when you push down on it; a mop I'll never use.

One orange bed stand with do-it-yourself screw-in legs; a CD-Radio-Alarm clock ("it has two timers!" Mom said); one sprisher of Fantastic, one vacuum-sealed package of smoked salmon; 32 cans of tuna fish; a trout; 12 paper towels; three rolls of laminated paper to insert in the bottom of drawers ("you don't know who lived here before!"); one foam egg crate to cushion the hard surface of the school-issued mattress; one mattress-cover to harden the cushy surface of the egg crate; plastic hooks.

That cream for the foot fungus.

Three posters to hang on the walls; two packs of putty with which to hang them; one bag of granola; one blue comforter; one pair of light-green sheets ("verdant!"); moisturizer ("Just wait until your skin cracks in the winter – then you'll thank me!"); two bookends; one bottle of seltzer; 10 energy bars; one pair of fleece earmuffs (see moisturizer); one tube of ChapStick; spindle of compact discs.

That drying powder one sprinkles on the scrotum.

The things we carried were largely determined by necessity, though my father protested this point – right up through his handing over of the silver credit card to my mother to swipe. They included, additionally:

A backup cell phone charger; one pair of headphones; two pumps of hand sanitizer, which smelled like vodka; three sticks of antiperspirant gel ("despite the fact that parabens may cause cancer"); a calendar; masking tape; one desk lamp; one stapler; one box of extra staples; one box of pens; four spiral notebooks; Febreze spray for the bathroom; one coffee-bean grinder ("but, Mom – do you know how much money I'll save by doing it myself?"); one atlas (Dad's idea – "a man needs to know how to get around"); three shrink-wrapped bundles of Charmin; plastic utensils; plates; cups; flypaper.

The things we carried were loaded on a Saturday night. I was on the cusp of moving into college, and not entirely appreciative of the fact – though grateful, nevertheless, I could use "cusp." I'd miss much about my hometown, but perhaps the road signs most of all, their improvised eroticisms – "NO TURN ON FRED" being but one – having always cheered me.

We woke early on Sunday. The sun was like a bath, to be entered. My dad drove and I sat shotgun, my mom in the back. We made good time. Stopping at New Jersey rest stations, we several times engaged in that state's unofficial pastime. From there it was farther South, and over the Delaware River, to reach Philadelphia and our destination. We followed the highway around the city's southern bend – a marshy heap paved over with stadiums – and up the highway next to the western river, the Schuylkill.

So you pull into campus – we pulled into campus. And I felt like I wanted to throw up. Not because the place intimidated me – because it was all gorgeous brick and very inviting (although somehow I had signed up online to live in a concrete high rise on the periphery of campus – I have no idea how that happened) – but because the air was slightly brisk. And I have this Pavlovian response. I associate it with school. I breathe in the crunchy leaves and the early dusk and something rises in my throat and I realize I should take a Prevacid or some other proton-pump inhibitor to stop the acid from fucking my esophagus. That's the first day of school. That's fall.

All the parked cars around us were popped open. Cords and cables spilled from their hatches, like the innards of a slit pig

****

"Well, I think that's it," Mom said, after she had washed the bathroom tiles.

"If we leave now, we can get back in time to watch Sunday night baseball," Dad said.

I smiled, thinking it was nice my parents would remain the same.

"Who's playing?" I asked. And then it hit me, unexpectedly, that I'd have to watch alone.

"Philly and Arizona. Shawn Green's gonna be back in the lineup."

"Ah, yes, the Jew. Was he injured?"

"No, no. His wife just gave birth. Second time."

"*Mazel tov.*"

My parents moved toward the door, and I followed. We walked down the stairs in silence (the elevator having long since exasperated us), and then out past the walnut trees. A branch brushed against my arm, like the bristles of a car wash.

"So this is it," Mom said, her voice high and cracking.

"Not at all. I'll walk with you guys to the garage."

My mom cried much less than expected at the car. Her eyes were moist, sure, and she pressed me against her and we hugged, but it didn't last as long as I had imagined it would, and she sounded confident and sure.

"You're going to have a great time," she said – but it wasn't spoken as a contrast, in the way that some parents do when what they really mean is, "You're going to have a great time, and here I am, middle-aged and dead-ended, forced to return home to a worn existence."

No, there wasn't envy in my mom's voice, and no pride either. She was merely contented, and after the long ride up – when I had urged her not to cry, it was a natural step, don't recall my nursery days, it'll just make it harder – I was shocked at her composure. I was like a boy who dumps a girl only to find himself utterly frustrated, after her initial distress, at her placid acceptance. My mom, supposed to lose control, had not.

I didn't want to create a scene – though on the roof of a five-story parking lot, it wouldn't have much mattered – but I also couldn't stand the thought of no scene: of normality, as if this were a natural step, as though the family were moving on.

The exhaust came out like a black scuff on a wooden floor. I called them not long after, to remind them to call *me*, once they got home.

They were like, "Of course," but then something came on over 1010 WINS and I'm sure my dad was looking at the clock, anticipating traffic on the 1s, and he'd give them their fucking 22 minutes, and in return, expectantly, he'd await the world.

So I just sat there, in my seat, thinking. And the Shawn Green comment came back to me. And I remembered in turn my first baseball game. I was high up – upper deck. And the Mets sucked. I think they gave up three leads in the first eight innings. And there were errors – probably Rey Ordonez trying to do something flashy on a routine grounder up the middle. But I'll never forget – top of the ninth, this fat guy with a transistor radio takes off his binoculars and hands them to me. And I press them to my cheekbones and I feel the cold plastic on my skin and then – 'cause it's fuzzy at first – boom – everything comes into focus. And I can see all the players, individually, standing with their gloves on the field.

It was amazing to me how – when you looked close – you realized how they never quit scratching themselves.

Sept. 1, 2005

Orientation still ongoing, I explored campus today, to get a better sense of this place I'll inhabit:

- The campus is bisected by an east-west thoroughfare named the Alley. It leads from the river on one side to the slummy neighborhood on the other from which we're encouraged to run. Along this path are lecture halls, frat houses (most were banished to the periphery for raising numbered placards to rate women), student help centers and cafes.

- If you stand at one end of the Alley and stare ahead, the cobblestones resemble small loaves of bread, newly removed from the oven. They seem to rise pillow-like and pop.

- If it is sunny, girls sunbathe on the grassy fields adjacent to the Alley.

- Something amazing happens when a girl lies down. Her breasts, under gravity's leveling, sink into themselves, expanding outward like melting ice, or cheese overflowed from a tuna melt. The best of them extend but so far, retaining the spherical form. Even as they ease down the ribs, they are bounded, like spreading seas held in by dunes.

- A girl stands. What does it look like now? It slopes ever so softly, its terminus a pointed nipple, and it resembles the Mediterranean curve, as the Middle East slides into Africa.

****

"You're never ready," said Kenny, the unofficial house manager, when I held up my hand. "That's not how it works. You do it, *then* you feel prepared."

I was declining a blunt, at my first party – an affair aptly advertised, by a sign over the door, as "40s and Blunt Night."

The frat, located at Beech and 41st, was an odd combination of the deeply textured and coldly smooth. The carpets were a rich, shaggy pile; the drapes a burgundy velvet. And yet on every wall – over mantels, on doors, in the foyer – were flat-screen televisions, as though arranged by some conceptual artist to loop footage of an excruciating scene – the skin-piercing plunge of a hypodermic needle, for instance.

That my mind was so wildly imaginative should not seem foolish. For this was a frat that, now unofficial, had earlier in the decade had its school license revoked for the kidnapping of another frat's president in a gasoline-doused blanket.

A curly-haired boy – his medicine-ball shoulders, bulbous and hard, stretching a cotton sweater – waddled toward Kenny.

"Isn't that college?" he said, his voice reedy and distant. "Not being prepared?"

"Yeah, Steff, yeah," said Kenny, laughing, smacking him between the shoulder blades, "that's college."

"It *is*, bro. It's all premature. College is fuckin' premature. Well, you know what? *Fuck* college."

This conversation ongoing, and looking likely to continue – their already slurred speech further attenuated by the Tetrahydro-cannabinol now bound to their brains – I walked upstairs, into a bedroom with a long mahogany desk, on top of which lay yet another flat-screen, its protective tape still affixed.

"Hey."

Turning around, I was confronted by a guy of medium height with rough stubble, a cleft chin and tortoise-shell glasses whom I recognized, though couldn't name, from the Jewish Center orientation.

"Oh, hey," I said, unwilling to ask his name for fear he might recall mine (which disparity would reflect poorly).

"What's going on in here?" I asked.

"Oh, nothing," he said, gesturing with his hand toward the bed. "There's a bottle of tequila over there, but the guy I was with – Mo is his name – he said he wouldn't do it without a lemon or a lime because it would turn his stomach. So I told him, if he wanted that so badly, he should go downstairs and get it himself."

"Yeah, that sounds like Mo," I said, only vaguely remembering who Mo was.

A tall guy entered the room clutching two fruits like baseballs and a blue cylinder of Morton's salt, the last of which – its label, an umbrella-toting girl, recalling my family home, where its ubiquity was matched only by Heinz – comforted me in what was, admittedly, a very foreign place.

"Oh, hey," he said, setting the lemons and the salt on the desk. "You go to the Jewish Center."

"Yes," I said. "We circumcised people tend to do that."

He screwed his face up as if puzzled. There goes that, I thought. Can't befriend a guy who doesn't like humor.

We moved into the half-light of the lamp hanging over the desk. I got a better sense of the guys. The medium height one wore a baseball cap – the compromise head-covering. He easily could have been a visiting professor – one of those precocious, scholarly guys who complete a PhD at the same time as a bachelor's and, by the age of 29, have assumed a tenured faculty position which, as evidenced in the envious looks of colleagues, is a stepping stone to the department chair. Already I noticed his habit of pinching his chin and his habit of nictitation – the way he blinked through life, almost as though trying to bring it into focus – like an old nickelodeon projector that flips through hundreds of still animations in order to vivify the story, to make it appear real. There was a calmness about him, a sense of being; he very clearly understood why he was here – in this house party, in this college, in this mode of existence, in which you spent the first quarter of your time (if you were ultimately lucky enough, that is, to reach 80) submitting to a rote education that may ill-suit you – and his movements and looks, the way every step of his sensible nubuck shoes seemed decided upon and considered, reminded me of the narration in a single-day novel – like "Mrs. Dalloway" or "Seize the Day" or "Saturday." Despite their shifts in fortune, the first-person protagonists of those stories always seemed so much more thoughtful than the rest of us. Of course, the more you read, the more you realized they were not – the author was simply making you aware of the processes you yourself were undergoing with each choice, the ones that had been subconscious until you, in a wild, vivid epiphany, realized you could slow it all down, could reduce the endlessly complex streams of life into a single, crystalline current.

Or perhaps I was getting ahead of myself. I do love speculation.

The tall one – Mo, I guess – had brown hair, similar in length and thickness to mine, only instead of being messed up with paste   so that it retained a rough matte look, so that it seemed haphazard and strewn about, a chunk poking up here, a chunk there – it was slicked forward and spiked up, with a shiny gel that, to my eye, oozed a decidedly meretricious luster. I was heartened, though, to see his head at least uncovered.

He wore a t-shirt that wasn't quite tight but still obtained an impression of his flesh. He had more of it than I did, it was obvious, yet he was still relatively slim, probably average for his size. I guessed, given the roundness of his features, the way they tended to fill out in happy little inflections, that he was a kind of jolly person, and wore pants size 34 x 34. He wore white leather sneakers and wide painter's jeans that, far from signaling a workman utility, indicated instead the great divide between his understanding of clothing – at whom it was targeted and what message its manufacturer intended it to send – and its true purpose. He was, comically, the rich kid who doesn't know it.

"So are we gonna do this, Vern?" he said.

"Yeah, but let's include – hey, what's your name again?"

"Jeremiah," I said, after a momentary pause. "I never told you."

"Oh, good. So…how is this done?"

"You mean you don't know?" Mo asked.

"How should I know?" said Vern. "Back where I come from, the only bottles we took out of the liquor cabinet were scotch. No self-respecting parent drinks tequila."

"Well, I don't know either."

"Maybe he knows."

They turned to me. The truth is, I did know, but just barely, and only because in the previous spring I had made out with my dad's secretary. As you may remember, we had happened upon the same bar coincidentally, and Patrón, sponsoring some event, had been holding an open bar (which is why our mutual presence there was no really no coincidence) of just tequila. I had watched carefully as she had licked her wrist and then done the same to mine. She had then shaken out the salt until it coated our arms like baby powder, and then we had rolled our tongues over the granules – I on her and she on me – and downed the shots and bit into the pulpy lemon wedges (at one point, I bit too hard and an acidic lump shot right in my eye).

Then when I had said bye and tried to hug her she had planted a wet one on me. So I hadn't forgotten what to do.

"Yeah, let me show you," I said, proud of assuming responsibility for the newly formed group. I laid out the materials on the flat-screen television (the effects of the 40 may have played a part in this) and poured out a small mountain of salt.

"What about the TV?" Vern asked.

"What about it?" I retorted. I was in charge now.

The other two did as I said and when we all bit into our lemons, our eyes met, all of us looking up to check whether the others were equally sour-pussed. It was small, no doubt, this shared ordeal, and yet it seemed to mean something that it was in fact shared, instead of alone, amidst strangers.

"Another?" Mo asked.

"Why not?" I said.

Vern looked around the room. It seemed groups kept shuffling in and, upon seeing a secretive, closed-off trio of guys in a corner, standing over a white powder on a television, kept shuffling out, hesitant to involve themselves.

"Don't you think we should offer some to everyone else?" he asked.

"Whose tequila is it?" I asked, eyeing the teal label.

"I dunno – I got it from downstairs."

"Well, let's just say it's been annexed."

Mo giggled. I was pleased.

Sept. 2, 2005

I told myself I wasn't gonna wallow when I bought this journal – that I'd be really journalistic and just write things as they happened, without bitching. But I gotta talk after meeting these guys.

Dunno how this will play out. I'm excited but also aware of what has happened.

Always been more comfortable talking to girls than boys. Why can be debated (and may be by professors, whose dissertations, encompassing the differences between Muenster and Havarti, have touched on topics more abstruse), but the odds – as has been the case with all character studies since Freud first purchased a mustache-trimmer – are on my father's rearing.

I mean, the man showed me, from the age of four, all these movies, from the 1970s – "10" and "Animal House" and all of Woody Allen's stuff. And I guess these should have benefited me. But I think instead of learning what it was to be a man in the presence of other men I learned what it was to be a man in front of women.

That's why I placed that ill-conceived love note in the jacket of Simone. A second-grader going after a fourth-grader. What was I thinking? First of all, she could have put on the jacket and not seen the note and gotten a paper-cut in the armpit; secondly, she was tall and beautiful at a time my friends were playing Pogs. She was nothing like a Pog. To think that I asked her – in a later note – to meet me at the *Aleph*[2] in front of school. And to think I waited.

---

[2] This is the first letter of the Hebrew alphabet. Jeremiah's elementary school had a beautiful red sculpture of the *Aleph* by its entrance.

I guess girls were easier. They were interested in the texture of life – the coarseness of a fabric, the solidity of a heel. What the fuck did you say to boys? I knew sports. But it was often in my discussion of sports that I tripped. I remember when we were in the fourth-grade we were talking about baseball. I said I had the utmost respect for Moses Fleetwood Walker, who in 1884 became the first black to play in the Big Leagues (a fact I had picked up from my dad's trivia book).

Yishai Noble, with one knee propped on the bench in the synagogue, objected.

"Like hell he was the first!" he shouted, his curly hair, against the dim sanctuary lights, like a black halo. "It was Jackie Robinson. My dad said so."

The other boys, kowtowing to Noble because of his brawn and older brothers, agreed.

"Well, the thing is," I began, already perceptive of my misstep. "Technically, Walker was the first. You see, the Jim Crow era—"

"Oh, hell," Yishai shouted again. "Here you are, claiming you know all this trivia, and you don't even know the first black player?"

He guffawed. The boys followed.

Their faces – creased in the same places – seemed threatening to me – as though hiding something sharp, like silk held together by pins.

"Yes, yes, but…"

I couldn't continue. My throat, suddenly dry, was cracking. Balls of heat were churning in my cheeks. I was terribly scared – though of what, I wasn't sure.

"C'mon, guys, let's go talk to someone who *actually* knows baseball," Yishai said, turning his back on the *Aron Kodesh* and marching out. And the pack followed, leaving me alone.

I cried that night – and frequently during my first school years. I was naturally athletic and not untalented – far from the gawky nerd my imaginary reader imagines – and possessed all the attributes to be accepted. But I was sensitive, with saran wrap skin – always being punctured. Every sight and sound (malign or not) moved me, stirred the source – cortex or vas deferens or whatever – of emotion.

Yes, it was openness that undermined my resolve and good sense (somehow, in the company of girls, that was a virtue). And even once I had metamorphosed into a steely-shelled specimen, in puberty, I still wouldn't befriend males; I was wary. Were there exceptions? Sure – but often they served to recall for me why I had avoided the gender in the first place. Take middle school. At that time, I invited guys to my house to sleep over. Sometimes it went well; but sometimes I didn't sleep right and got hit in the nose with a Nerf ball. Or take high school. There I was popular and well-liked but still found myself confounded. Once, I went with a friend to the Garden on a Saturday night to see a fight. And there we were, sitting not far from the ring, during the undercard, when who should come take a seat in the row before us but Tito Trinidad. And my buddy and I – it was Lenny – we went to piss before the main event, both wide-eyed at our great fortune, to be sitting so near such an acclaimed fighter, and we sidled up to the urinals – which were not partitioned – and I said what I was honestly and innocently thinking: "Wow. I never realized how good-looking Trinidad is." And Lenny hushed me and looked away – aware of how dangerous such a statement was – of how any profession canvassing Trinidad's looks, no matter how platonic the speaker's intent, could get us pummeled.

I was so humiliated – my cheeks were red. How had I not realized what I was saying?

But it was just an observation. I would've said the same if it had been Tito's wife.

No, it was never a gay thing. Sitcoms and movies – an entire genre nicknamed Bromance – would have us believe this is the main source of tension between buddies. The homosexual subtext.

Bullshit.

There are bigger problems. I had 'em. Ambition: Every Shabbos, after services had ended, and lunch had been consumed, the high school boys in my neighborhood would gather on a grassy field in the middle of an intersection – it was wonderfully triangular – to play softball. At first, I joined them, eager to get out and swing a bat. But as freshman year progressed, and the pressure of contemporary, Manhattan-based private-schooling got to me, I began to fear I was wasting my time. The games went on for hours, I reasoned, and occurred every week, and cumulatively, those sessions, if spent poorly, might come back to haunt me, later on in college and then further down the road in my 20s, when my vocabulary might not be as comprehensive as others', my sentences not as crisp (which fear also manifested itself in a disturbing dream, wherein Henry James sliced paper cuts into his nostrils with a copy of "Daisy Miller"). Oh, how I desperately wanted to become a writer.

So I quit the game. And spent the remainder of my high school Saturdays – forbidden by Sabbath rules from using electricity – reading the dictionary. I found, among other things, that the slang term "douche bag" had originated in 1963 (and that its use, therefore, in Woody Allen's "Radio Days" was anachronistic)

Malice: Quite simply, some boys exhibited an undue meanness, and this never failed to surprise me. Why? I always asked. Michael Schoenfeld, who played with me at recess, jumped me from behind and punched me in the face (kindergarten); Yonah Klein, a new kid whom I had warmly accepted into the grade, requited my affection by placing pickles under my trousers as I took my seat (third grade); Ross Cohen, a usually amiable boy, screamed at me on the basketball court (seventh grade, and it was his fault, the schnitzel-faced bastard – he had thrown the ball inbounds very poorly and it had gone way, way over my head; I wasn't fucking Gumby).

Oh, man – I can't help remembering now. My mind is hot tea – swirling with the honey and sugar I try pouring in but weighed down, on the bottom, by the dregs.

Differing perspectives: Saved this for last, because it may be super important. In high school, I began to think differently. Whereas other guys took certain facts about the gender for granted – that they simply *had* to have other guy friends; and that this need could be satisfied by mutual experience, by the watching of a game together, or the riding of a roller-coaster – I questioned both the necessity of male bonding and the methods by which it was ostensibly achieved.

On the first count, I wondered what function male friendship served – or really, any friendship at all, for by this point, I had already drifted from most of my girl friends and pursued that sex solely on a romantic basis. For spiritual companionship, I reasoned, I could turn to these girlfriends (as no boys would ever mean as much to me as a hottie); for intellectual stimulation, I similarly argued, I could read books (as no boy – at least none I knew – would ever match Zola). And so I failed to see what time among buddies provided – what phenomenon took place, during the hours of video games and basketball, that might justify the tedium of those activities

What can I say? I loved video games and basketball – I just didn't see what the people provided. Mutual experience didn't seem enough. It seemed a huge deception. We'd talk – us guys – in the locker room about Mara Filstein's tight ass and shiny red hair. And we'd appear to be involved in each other's lives. But then we'd peel off to different places and study alone, at home, in the dark.

What the fuck was that? Where were the sounds volleying from other houses? Like, "Hey, Jeremiah. My homework sucks. Isn't existence futile?"

Would've been nice to hear. Not hearing it, I guess I stopped thinking it was necessary or possible. Sometimes I thought telling each other stories might help.

Sept. 9. 2005

"Whoops," Mo said, breaking into a wide, boyish smile – an intentionally innocent grin, meant to disarm me.

I looked at him hard.

He had just spread food bits all across the blue surface of my bed. It looked similar in color and composition to the Hudson River in winter, when jagged crumbs of ice float on the turbid, squally water. But this was no river.

Your bed in school is sacred. What more space do you have? And my mom had made it when she moved me in.

He hadn't even been invited, but had rather called at 7:55 to invite himself. "Where are you?" I had asked. I had believed him to be still in the Quad, in the room he shares with another Atlanta boy. "Outside your door," he had said. And then he had entered, jumped on my bed, and pulled a bag of tortilla chips from an adjacent shelf. He popped it open and they spilled and he accidentally rolled over them with his ass.

"I have to sleep there, *man*," I said now, drawing out the last word.

"Geez, Jeremiah. It's just chips. Calm down."

"Calm down?" I slurred the words.

"But that's my bed. I sleep there. Or at least, I try to. Now I'm gonna roll over onto fragmented corn chips."

"Tortilla. They're not corn."

"Tortilla chips are made of corn, and even if they weren't, I still lie there, right where your nasty socks are. Hey! Get them off the pillow."

He lifted his feet off my uneven pillow – which for whatever reason bulges on its right side – with raised eyebrows and outstretched hands, as if to say, Sorry, didn't think this would offend you.

He has no concept of personal space, I thought. He wasn't even invited.

And then I thought – Jesus – why are you mad? You're already blowing it.

"Let's just watch the game, eh?"

I pried myself from the seat and flipped on the television. I asked him about his father – whether they watched games on Sundays in their house as I did with my dad in mine – and he demurred, saying something about health and 66 years of age. "He prefers studying plants."

We began picking up the chips; I grabbed one and was about to put it in my mouth when I wondered what he would think. He stuffed his face with them.

"They're still good."

"Couldn't agree with you more," I replied, grabbing some by his knee cap. I was back in.

Just then a loud knock came from the door.

"Well, aren't you going to get it?"

"Yeah, yeah. I'm coming!"

He remained on the bed as I walked down the short hall.

I twisted the knob.

"Ah, finally!" said Vern, who had on olive chinos and a striped sweater, *The Language of the Self* pinned by his elbow against his ribs. "I thought I'd finish all of Lacan before you got here."

"Sorry." He slid his way by me, into the hall and I wondered how he knew where I lived.

"Mo said I should come. He said you'd be watching."

"No worries – have some chips – you'll find them on the bed."

Vern sat on a chair and stuck his nose back in Lacan.

"Are you not gonna watch?" The thought of him reading instead of being with guys – that thing I had always done – freaked me.

"Nah, I don't really care for it. I just want to hang."

RAP-RAP-RAP.

Another knock.

Who could that be?

I walked down the hall, opening the door to reveal not one, not even two, but three different girls. I recognized them from the Jewish Center but could not come up with names.

"Oh, um, heyyyyy…*girls*."

The first one – tall, with wavy black hair, and a piece of gum clicking in her mouth like castanets – was the first to enter.

"Oh, hey, Jeremiah. Mo said you guys would be here. So we came by."

"I see." How did she know my name?

She walked past me inside and then the two other girls followed.

The first, a shorty in a plaid blouse and jeans, I already had heard was a really talented gossip (someone had probably gossiped that to me). No – actually, I *had* spoken to her – on Shabbos morning, after shul. I remembered thinking she was a really good storyteller. Kinda freaked me.

Then the third girl.

It was her.

Big brown eyes, long brunette hair with flashes of red, a tiny nick on the bottom of one of her teeth – not big or farmer-like – just kind of exciting (think Sarah Jessica Parker's mole). I had been watching her in Spanish seminar. For a week now. She wore skirts and moccasins and was clearly *shomeret negiah*[3].

Have you ever looked at someone and immediately imagined they were everything you weren't seeing?

Made no fucking sense – but I saw her each day, in her headbands and blouses, and pictured her staying up really late with me and disobeying her parents' orders and getting yelled out and then running back to my house and finding me there, in the basement, and then snuggling with me in mussed up sheets on a futon while Comedy Central played in the background.

"Well, aren't you going to let me in?" she asked.

I was standing right in front of her.

"Oh, yeah. Sorry."

She smiled, then walked away.

****

The tall one was named Rosie.

"I don't wanna watch football."

Mo waved at her with her hand so she would step aside from the TV. I was sitting in the corner, by the closet, cross-legged on the floor. Aliza was next to me. She had grabbed a pencil from my desk.

"Here."

I watched her draw boxes on the bottom of the white painted wall. And then make a big x in the middle.

"You're 'o.'"

"Oh, am I?"

"Yes. And I am going to fuck you up."

---

[3] *An observer of the injunction not to touch the opposite sex.*

I could not believe those words had just left her pretty mouth.

"Game on," I said, grabbing the pencil.

****

"Have you guys seen this?" Shani said. Shani was the short gossip. She started reading from the school newspaper.

"All freshmen who want to apply for the final columnist position must submit a sample piece by Tuesday night – the 13th."

Of course I had seen it.

"I hadn't seen that," Mo said. He grabbed the paper from her.

He scanned it quickly. Shani snatched it back.

"Mo," said Rosie. "You were a newspaper geek in high school, weren't you?"

"Huh?" He looked up from his twiddling thumbs. "Yeah. I was."

Aliza said it was really hot and unbuttoned the top button of her blouse. It wasn't a fancy shirt – just a cowboy snap-button thing – and nothing was revealed. But still a spunky move.

"The newspaper kids are supposedly wild," Shani said. "Their parties are crazy."

Mo had grabbed my pillow and was hugging it.

****

There had been two stalemates and she had won the third game.

"I concede," I said.

"Don't sweat it." Aliza pat the floor by my knee – but didn't make contact. "You'll get better. In time."

"It's true," Rosie said to Mo. "And not just that, but there's a writing instructor here – a novelist, I mean, who teaches classes. He also takes on individual kids."

"I've heard of him," Vern said. He was still reading, but also talking.

"Harkinson, Helfington – something like that."

"It's Hutchinson." Rosie sounded like she knew better. I think her brother had been here. "Len Hutchinson. He's working on a novel now about writers on performance enhancing drugs. There's a government investigation."

"Jeremiah doesn't have a fucking chance," Mo said. I didn't know what he was talking about – barely heard – but it sounded like a pen-prick.

****

"Favorite movie?" I asked.

"Easy," she said. "'Love and Death.'"

"'Love and Death?' Are you serious?"

"Yeah, why?"

"Because, well…wow – 'Love and Death.' That's perfect." Because it was – it was perfect.

"I watched a lot with my older brothers – and my dad," Aliza said.

****

Aliza was the only one left. Curled up, like a cat, on my bed.

"So this is it?" she said. She was looking at an Entertainment Weekly cover I had hung up.

"I'm not a great decorator."

"You read EW?"

"Why not?"

Such chatter continued. All the while, my mind roamed elsewhere, into the various ways the situation could have come to pass. She was beautiful. Her cowboy top was loose like a chemise, her butt hugged by the jean skirt.

"What do you think of Spanish?" I asked.

"I probably don't think it's as easy as you."

"Why do you say that?"

"You know what's going on – I can tell."

"So you've been looking away from the board."

"Oh, my gosh – how can I not? It's sooo boring."

"You know she threatened to fail me."

"Really?"

"Yup."

"Why?"

"The New York Times."

"Well, yeah! You're sooo obvious."

"What do you suggest I do to pass the time?"

"You could text someone."

"That costs money. And who would I text that early?"

And so it progressed – not on deep terms or with an immediate trust, because I had just met her. And she was on my bed.

It turned out she had grown up in a suburb of this city, maybe 30 minutes from the campus, but, like most kids from the area, had rarely ventured in. It was an existence of cul-de-sacs and Acura Legends– the concrete cracked with varicose veins.

"Do you like puppies?" she asked. "Because I have this whi—"

"No."

"Oh. Because I have this white little thing, he has the cutest little—"

"So you do. They're not really my thing."

"You don't like animals?"

"Not really, no."

"What do you like?"

"People — but very few."

"That's kind of you."

"Thank you."

The mock formality — "thank you"s and "you're quite welcome"s — continued. They were all embarrassment-modifiers. At a certain point, say 30 minutes in, I began to wonder how it would end. I didn't want her to leave — although I was running out of topics and the nervousness of the thing began to exceed the pleasure — but I had to take a major dump and was unsure I could hold it.

"Look at the wind outside," she said. "It's gonna blow the building over."

My stomach felt like it was going to drop out. I had to go now.

"Excuse me — I'm just gonna go use the restroom."

I bolted from the bedroom and slammed the door of the bathroom. I landed on the toilet hard. I grabbed for the knob. Gotta flush now — to drown out the sound of the...

TOO LATE. I roared.

I exited minutes later. I felt I needed to say something quickly — to cover up the fact that I had been in there so long and had clearly taken a shit. Not that it would be a real cover, but...

"So you watched Woody Allen with your dad?"

She didn't answer. She looked wounded. "I really don't want to talk about it," she said. And then, after some silence, "I'm gonna leave."

I had no idea what I had done.

Sept. 26, 2005

The Saturday-night game against Dupont – our team's first of the season – started before *Shabbos* was over, but we went afterward and got there in time for the second quarter. It was cold and I was wearing the school sweater I had purchased from the Barnes and Noble-owned bookstore. Mo was wearing the exact same sweater only in the reverse colors.

"Where'd you get that?" I asked.

"Probably where you got yours," he said. He sped up, leaving me with Vern, who was carrying *Thus Spake Zarathustra*.

"You're bringing that?"

"No. I just like carrying it."

He opened it up.

Behind us were the girls. I kept hearing snippets of the conversation. I imagined it was about me.

"If it isn't Pepto-Bismol."

I froze. The voice was Rosie's, which meant Aliza had told her about my long crap. And Shani knew – and Shani told everyone. They were all there.

"Haha," I said.

Rosie ran ahead.

"I'm sorry," Aliza said.

I didn't know how to respond. We hadn't spoken since the Woody Allen question.

"I'm not embarrassed – don't worry."

Lies.

Shani told me not to worry, it once happened to her when she was on a date *also* and she wouldn't tell a soul. Aliza was smiling. I kept thinking on that word – "also."

****

Did I mention there is another girl? An older one? And that she was at the game?

In time.

****

The buildings on either side of us seemed to loom over the campus, like ancient custodians.

"I swear, they're watching us," Aliza said. We passed the green brick of the campus' original buildings. The first, at 36th, was originally the Medical Hall and now housed humanities classes. The second had once been a gymnasium but now contained admissions and the literary society, which occupied the attic. There was a light on up there. Vern looked up from his book.

****

We could hear it, the sound of cheers and horns and songs, and we walked faster. We jogged past the statue of the school founder and the library. The more we ran the more we had to stop.

"Slow down!" Shani said.

"It's the first game!" Mo called back. Rosie was holding onto his arm. I wouldn't say he was resistant, but from behind him, I could see him veer.

****

Mo pointed to an empty bench half way up.

"Let's just sit," Shani said. We walked. The higher we climbed the more we could see. There were four guys in the front row standing shirtless. They had the school's nickname painted on their bellies.

"I'm freezing," Aliza said. She was sitting between Mo and me.

Should I give her my sweatshirt? Would she take it?

"Jeremiah? Is that you?"

I turned around. It was Caroline, the WASPy senior columnist who had given me a tour of the newspaper office. I had submitted my application to the editor and then she had taken me, room to room, languorously – as Cleopatra, in her palace, might have Mark Antony once.

"Oh, hey…" I said.

What else do you say, when you want to say, "I'm really excited to be sitting next to you at a football game" but also sitting next to you at a football game is another girl you want to say that to?

"It's good to see you."

She looked at me with the full authority of her 21-year-old gaze, indifferent to Aliza's presence.

"Have you heard anything from the newspaper?"

"No."

She nodded.

"I'll let you get back to the game."

Our quarterback found his favorite receiver for a 53-yard touchdown – to put us up 17-7. The cheerleaders, per tradition, did a pushup for each of the team's points and the fans counted out every one. The band, too, struck up a traditional cheer, whose final refrain demanded more points. And the belly-painted freshmen led a raucous spelling of the school's name.

Then we turned it over a bunch of times. Where was the fat man and his binoculars?

"They suck," Mo said to Rosie. His hand was in her lap.

"*You* could do a better job," she said.

They both went to the concession stand.

****

"So that girl can help you at the newspaper?" Aliza asked. No one in our row or the one behind us was around.

"I think so," I said. "I'm trying to curry favor."

What I actually think:

- She has light blue eyes.

- She attended an all-girl's high school, on breaks from which, driving to the shore, she hung out with boys named Tad.

- Doing a dual degree in the college and business school, she is doubly knowledgeable.

- She admires my writing.

The second half was a slow grind whose conclusion we all foresaw. Our team kept giving up easy passes, and on offense, though we managed to dink and dunk, no drives materialized. It was obvious we were heading to a close finish – one that would be ours if time would only run out before our team's energy. It did not – and so, Dupont taking a 28-24 lead, we received the ball to begin our final drive with 2:51 on the clock.

How much of my shitting had she heard?

The shouting from the crowd was fierce. Even more than before the wind seemed to whip us, increasing the frenzy we hoped would carry down onto the field and propel our players.

"I'm nervous," Shani said.

"Shut up," Rosie said, in a nervous way.

The first three plays resulted in an eight-yard gain, leaving our team with a fourth-and-two at its own 33.

"LET'S GO!" roared the half-naked freshmen.

And as one, our section stood up, except Vern..

"Damn it, Vern!" I said. I slapped him on the shoulder. "You gotta get up! This is it."

"Oh."

He jumped to his feet and let the book fall to the floor. Shocking.

"Hold my hand!" Aliza said. Did she know what she was saying?

Hell yeah, I did it.

The ball was hiked, through the center's legs to the quarterback, who was in the shotgun. He looked left and found no one, and then right and found no one, and was finally grabbed by a Dupont linebacker and sacked.

"Sonofabitch!" Mo said. Our entire section sagged back to the seats.

"I can't believe it," Rosie said.

Aliza began to say something but I couldn't hear it. A voice came over the PA system.

"Penalty on the field. Defense. Facemask. Fifteen Yards. First Down."

As one again, the student section rose. The band played "The Final Countdown."

Aliza grabbed my hand.

"LET'S GOOOO!" screamed the half-naked freshmen.

And go the team did – backwards – losing a cumulative three yards on three plays to force a fourth-and-thirteen with 14 seconds left.

"They call this football?" Vern yelled. It was a surprise. "They suck. It's pathetic."

"There's still one play left," I said. "And maybe two, if they play it right."

Before we knew it the ball had been snapped – this time from Dupont's 45 – and once again our quarterback was scanning the field, seeing no open receivers, evading linemen. He was about to be sacked. It would end the game. Aliza gasped. So did Caroline (I could hear her). And then, suddenly, the QB chucked the ball – to avoid being hit – into the spiraling wind. It was heading out-of-bounds. But it was redirected – into the hands of a receiver at the three yard line,. He fell and was downed. A catch!

"Fuck yeah!" said Mo. Vern grinned like a little boy. Rosie was clutching the ends of her sweatshirt. There were five seconds left on the clock. The team had one play left, from three yards away.

"What are they gonna do?" Shani asked. She turned to Vern.

"I dunno," he said. He turned to me.

"I don't know," I said. The running back had gotten injured earlier in the game.

The play was off. Again the ball spiraled from the center's *tuchus*, again the quarterback gripped it. Again his receivers were covered.

I felt Aliza's hand.

The quarterback rolled to his right. If no one was going to help him, he'd have to do it himself. He planted one foot to the outside and then another, cutting toward the orange pylon just a few yards away. He was clear – all the backs and safeties were in the center of the field. He lowered his head, as if to reduce drag. Three more strides – that was all he needed.

Whoosh. That was one.

Whoosh. He turned the corner.

CRUNCH! He was tackled from behind by a nandrolonal beast – a hulking shoulder pad which contained a person.

The quarterback lay motionless on the ground.

The fans lay motionless on their seats.

"I really thought we had it," Vern said. "I really did."

All you could hear were sighs.

Then, suddenly, my name.

"Jeremiah," said Caroline. She leaned over from her row. "Don't get upset. Our team always sucks."

I didn't know what she was hinting at and I saw Aliza in my peripheral vision. Caroline leaned in closer. Then she kissed me on the cheek.

"You'll get over it," she said. She walked out of the row, down the stairs.

My phone started ringing. I wanted to get it but I also wanted to say something – Aliza was staring at me – and so were Mo and Rosie and Vern and Shani. Their huge collective jaw was on the floor.

"I heard and smelled everything," Aliza said to me. She walked away. The other girls followed her.

"Pick up your phone, dude" Mo said.

I snapped to and grabbed it.

It was the newspaper. I had gotten the column.

Sept. 29, 2005

The first time she came to my apartment, she giggled and said she had something to show me on the Internet. In my mind, I heard then the shrill violins of the Berlin Philharmonic's rendition of "Rock You Like a Hurricane." But my excitement was misdirected. She opened a Web page with an archive of black-and-white public service announcements from the 1950s. "Isn't this great?" she asked. I nodded blankly. "Here, look," she said. And she played a video of little blonde boys performing the "duck and cover" drill under their desks, in preparation for a potential nuclear attack. They looked like turtles receding into their shells. And I understood then that what excites a girl like Caroline is unlikely to be the same thing that gets me.

She arranged this herself at the first meeting (that I attended, at least) of the seven newspaper columnists. To one of the juniors, she extended an invitation to play squash. To me, after I said something rather keen (about the necessity of good reporting, even for an opinion piece), she extended an invitation to go running. I don't know why. From that point on which is to say, for the past couple days we've been exchanging messages – on the phone, on the computer – with coy stuff. Nicholas Kristof goes a long way to wooing such a girl, though as I said, she scares me shitless.

She did compliment me – did like my prose – yet not as an equal but as a teacher, as someone trying to encourage a protégé instead of a partner.

So she was in my room, showing me the PSA, and she sat in the desk chair and I bent over her, peering at the screen over her shoulder. And she said, "Sit" – it was an order – and stood up. And I took her place on the little swivel recliner the school had provided with the room, and she lowered herself onto my lap and turned her head back toward mine.

"You're the kind of guy I could date, but three years," she said, "well – that's much too much."

We hung out anyway, and my hopes rose when she called me over to her group house one night. Ping-pong, it turned out, was the reason. She was in the mood to play. Another time, I was invited over to find a great big group watching a documentary on the history of race relations at the university. "I thought you'd find it really interesting," she said a couple days later.

Here, I must pause. Since I only update this journal periodically – and I haven't for a few days – it may seem I exaggerate. How could all of the above have occurred within a few weeks? So asks the mystical, nonexistent reader, who one day, in some other venue and with the work somehow transmuted into real literature, will hopefully be. The answer is simple – but worth noting:

Time passes differently in college.

Because all the boundaries are blurred – between home and work and play – because you live in the same building as the people you date, because you eat with the people in your class, because you do homework at 4 in the morning and you fall asleep at 4 in the afternoon – time loses the concrete markers with which we elsewhere measure it.

There we were, in the 50-degree night, standing outside the gym, stretching our calf muscles. I was doing everything she did. She was wearing tight black spandex pants and a fleece that zipped up to the collar. I was in a t-shirt with the sleeves cut-off and blue basketball shorts that read "Game Over" in white block lettering on the butt. I had gotten them from a basketball camp, but they still made me feel insecure.

"I haven't run in awhile," she said. "Probably don't have the stamina."

"I've never run," I said. "I find it boring."

"Yeah, after cross-country in high school, so did I."

Shit.

"I do go to the gym – I just lift."

"I hate guys like that. They're not even in shape. It's just a façade."

Shit.

We took off eastward on the bridge over the river. We passed streetlamps that gave off a dimmed glow and those that were just broken. We stepped onto cracked sidewalks and those bulging with the roots of nearby trees. We entered the cute, café part of the city, weaving through tables and chairs, under red awnings. We smelled crusty Italian bread fresh from the oven and menthol smoke of cigarettes. We skirted a mob of 20-somethings pouring out of a bar and dodged stumbling drunks hailing a cab. We felt the pounding bass from a club and caught a couple kiss inside a coupe. Caroline's ponytail bounced on her neck.

Don't think distance, I told myself. Moment at a time.

I tried to muffle the sounds of my deep, sucking breaths.

"I've never (breath) been (breath) to this (breath) part of the city."

"Really?"

We looped north-west to return to campus. I'd made it halfway. We passed brownstone walkups. They must host interesting dinner parties, I thought. Maybe Caroline has been—

Hey, where is Caroline?

She wasn't to my right. She wasn't to my left. Turned around – she was 20 feet behind me, leaning over a staircase, propped against the red brick.

"What's wrong?"

"I dunno. It's just—"

Blaach.

I watched her spray the building with half-digested chunks. It was unexpected.

"Are you okay?"

No answer.

Slowly, she straightened herself and turned back to me. Her face was pale. "Yeah," she said, her voice squeaky. "I think I'm better now."

I saw a cab coming our way. I motioned it toward us.

"Let's keep going," she said.

"No," I said, "I don't think we should. I'll pay for the cab. It's not a big deal."

"No, really," she said, letting out a forced giggle. "I'm *fine.*"

"Okay."

I shook my head. We slowly resumed our strides.

A few minutes later I looked down at her and smiled. She looked away. "That was ironic," I said.

We reached the bridge. A breeze skimmed the river's surface. It was calm.

"Hold on," she said. Her light blue eyes looked glossy.

She doubled over and grabbed the railing of the bridge. She made a scratchy coughing sound – maybe the acid burning her throat – and went, "Blaahch," hurling herself forward, a pinkish glop plunking into the river.

A moment passed.

"I dunno what's wrong with me," she said, wiping her mouth on her sleeve. "This never happens."

So after a moment more, we jogged ahead. When we got to the gym, I waved goodbye and told her to feel better, having forgotten the hug I had prepared myself to give. I shuffled off toward my apartment, wearing a great big bemused grin – which didn't leave my face – not as I pried the shirt off my sticky back, not as I showered, not as I crawled into bed.

In the great game of college life, I was now even on the grossness scale. One girl I liked had heard me shit and the other I had watched vomit. I missed the girl who had heard me shit.

Sept. 30, 2005

"Anyway, let's head out," Mo said. "The wind's only going to pick up – especially by the river."

Vern and I followed, down the Beech Street sidewalk.

I couldn't believe we were actually doing it. I felt like my reputation was on the line.

"I haven't room to fit a book in my jacket," Vern said.

It seemed as if it might rain. Vern and I caught up to Mo, who had mysteriously stopped, in front of the Wawa. This is where people who live in the Quad go to get nacho chips, I thought. When they're drunk. On Saturday nights.

(I should never have signed up for that high-rise. Or had I been placed there. By someone who knew me better.)

"Why, thank you so much," Mo said.

I noticed a small girl to his left. She was wearing a black shawl.

"No, really, I mean it. That piece you did, on the people in the lounge was great."

Mo tried to step away.

"I gotta keep walking. These guys are waiting for me."

"And it wasn't just funny," the girl continued. "It was also romantic."

"Thanks. I appreciate it. It was nice speaking to you…"

"Cindy."

"Cindy. It was nice speaking to you. Cindy."

We walked away. Mo poked Vern in the gut, as I hung back a little.

"You see that, boys? People do read the fucking alternative paper."

Apparently, I thought. The competitive thing was burbling up.

"They read the fucking alternative paper, and they see my column."

We passed all the restaurants on Beech Street. This is where students in the Quad go to eat lunch, I thought. When they're sober. On weekdays.

There was the Chinese place, the salad bar, the panini press and the cheese steak grill. The diesel generators of the food carts thrummed like giant cicadas.

We passed the student union.

"You're Mo Gross, right?"

The three of us turned around. Standing behind us was a short, skinny boy.

"Yes."

Vern looked at me. We knew what was coming.

"I just wanted to say, I really like your column."

Mo grinned.

"What can I say?" he said. "I try."

Mo, Vern and I continued down Beech Street, past the auditorium at 34th.

"Yeah, boys," Mo said. He was loud. "My shit is the shiznat."

I felt nauseated. It was one thing not to have someone read my stuff. But this...

We continued past the chemistry lab and anthropology museum. All the while Mo kept marveling at how insane it was.

We crossed the bridge over the river and descended to its east bank. The algae-green water, muddy and thick, foamed at the edges like beer.

"Where do we begin?" I asked.

Mo, ignoring me, kicked up a pile of dirt with the rubber edge of his Adidas. He watched it rise and fall, as sand that's been sliced by an errant golf swing. The small grains catching light, and reflecting it, were like little firecrackers.

"I don't buy it," he said.

"Look, I'll grant you it's far-fetched," I said. "But why would I ever make it up?"

"For attention."

"I don't need your fucking attention."

Whoa – why was I cursing?

"Whoa – why are you cursing?" Mo said.

"We're here to search for the vomit," Vern said. He pointed to the water. "Let's not fight."

"But Caroline!" I said. I was still loud. "Of all people, she'd be the least likely to throw up in the river. I would never make it up."

"That's the point. You knew how far-fetched the story was. You knew we'd have to believe it."

"You're insane."

I gave him a shove. I don't know why – I didn't think it was that hard.

He shoved back – *hard*. My legs slipped out from under me. I sprawled back. I paddled the air with my arms. And then:

Plash!

I was in the muddy thickness below. I couldn't breathe. I pushed down on the water. I surfaced. "Hu, hu, hu," I gasped.

"Do you see anything in there?" Mo said.

He laughed – an evil, grinning laugh. Vern shook his head.

Oct. 6, 2005

The table was silent but for sucking – the sound of chunks being swallowed. The sweet-mushroom-smell of chicken marsala, like a girl's perfume, curled its way up my nostrils. Rosh Hashanah dinner.

"Tell us about your friend," my mom said.

I rolled my eyes.

"Can't I eat for a moment? I promise I'll tell you everything."

"Just tell us," my mom said.

I liked Mo, but he brought out the competitiveness in me, which was bad because competitiveness had stopped me from befriending guys before and I really thought I had a chance with Mo, of all guys. There was something about him. Though he wouldn't open up.

"I like Mo," I said. "But he can be fucking annoying."

My younger brother laughed. My father scowled.

"Jeremiah – c'mon. That language is filthy."

My mother put a hand on his wrist.

"Shhh," she said. She nodded toward the hall.

"It's just not cool," he continued. "I know you hear this stuff in school, but you can't speak like that."

"But it's true," I said. "He *can* be fucking annoying."

"That's it!" my dad roared. "You're in big trouble when—"

He was trying to gesture to the hallway but his wrist bumped into his glass and his glass fell to the floor.

CRACK.

It spidered into a hundred tiny shards.

Just then Mo walked back in from the bathroom.[4]

---

[4] The Goldsteins were graciously hosting me for Rosh Hashanah because I could not make it back to Atlanta in time after my final class. Also, I really

"Did something shatter?" he asked.

didn't want to see my dad in his enfeebled, sickly state. That – on a holiday like this – would be too hard.

Nov. 6, 2005

The air had turned.

It was no longer jacket-optional or long-sleeves-after-sundown. It was frigid. Your hands, alligator-like, cracked. Your eyes, at the corners, stung. Your penis, in the shower, receded. Farther. But it was not winter. Wasn't nearly that calm. No lush snow, covering everything, unified it. No lights, decking windows, made them shine.

There were no songs, or shopping deals.

It was fall – violent, fickle fall – which, swirling through one part of campus and then the next – never paused to let you settle.

I kept begging her on the phone.

"Please – do something with me. It doesn't have to be major."

But Aliza wouldn't budge. She hung up pretty quickly. And when she didn't, I just felt worse.

"Been to any football games lately?" she asked.

It was already getting to be basketball season.

Finally, one day, she said yeah – we can go out on Sunday. To a museum. I said, sure, a museum, I love museums, which museum, do they have a café?

The last question was a joke. But after I said it I realized it could be misconstrued. 'Cause there's no way Aliza eats out.[5]

I felt like it was a test. We crossed the street, passing the Eero Saarinen-designed dorm. She seemed upset.

"Obviously you're upset."

"No."

_____

[5] This phrase is used by religious people to refer to the consumption of non-kosher food outside the home, which is seen somehow as more permissible or less sinful.

I said she was. She said, please change the subject. I said, remember that time I had terrible diarrhea? She didn't laugh.

At some point I just cracked.

"Geez. For how long are you gonna hold this against me? I don't even like her. *She* kissed me!"

"What?" She seemed puzzled. "What are you talking about?"

"You know. The kiss."

"No, no."

She rushed forward. I followed.

"Tell me."

"Fine." She sounded sharp and I was afraid of the news. "You wanna know? I hooked up with someone."

It hit me hard. I managed to ask when. She said last week. I said which was last week. 'Cause it was Sunday, which some people consider part of the previous week, 'cause in college the weekend is just a huge party to cap things off. And she said, no – I mean yesterday – Saturday.

Saturday? I asked. As in Shabbos?

It was in *shul*,[6] she said.

She wouldn't say who the guy was. I had my suspicions.

"I didn't want to go out with you like this," she said.

"Like what?"

"Like right after I did this. Because I can't look at you now."

She walked away and raised her fingers to hail a cab.

****

I had to pee.

---

[6] Synagogue.

she moved toward her bed, I thought of the guy
d on Shabbos. She must have also. Her phone was
nd she was scrolling through some sort of list.
up in your room," she said. She was looking at the
see you later."

We were in the 19th-century European Art gallery. I had shooed the cab away; we had entered the museum. I kept thinking how ironic the whole thing was. For a girl I liked I kept fucking things up. Just last week — this week, actually, 'cause it was last night, but it was after midnight, so technically it was today, Sunday — I had been with Caroline. I was playing ping-pong in her house — as I had done many times earlier. She asked me to her room. I followed. We found the bed.

"You're cute," she said. She nuzzled into me.

And we spooned — our bodies, neatly stacked, like plastic Solo cups. Now, I felt guilty. Though officially, Aliza and I weren't dating. And Aliza had just hooked up in *shul* — on Shabbos — did I even know this girl? — and Mo — what a righteous bastard — always bragging about his alternative column. Why was I thinking of Mo?

"The bathroom's down there," Aliza said.

I rushed. My bladder was a heavy water-balloon.

"Sorry, sir, you can't enter."

I turned. A security guard.

"Why not?"

He shook his head.

"Closed for cleaning. You'll have to use the American wing."

"Where's that?"

"Downstairs. Other side of the museum."

Not sure I could hold it, I asked him where the nearest Duchamp was. He stared. So I ran — past several impressionist pieces and some Barbizons.

****

On my way back, I noticed Caroline. She was surveying an Eakins.

"You didn't think you could pass me without saying hi, did you?" she said.

"No."

I had hoped I could. She was the last person I wanted to see. Why the fuck was *she* here? I had just asked her the night before what her Sunday plans were. She had been super vague. 'Cause if I had known she'd be at the museum, I would've stayed in the museum café, with Aliza.

"Isn't this great? It's just a study, but look at the balance between light and dark, and the hint of red. It's perfect."

"Yeah."

Still bashful.

"I don't have any patience for people who prefer the Europeans without even giving this a look. It's pretentious, to drop names like Monet without looking."

I nodded. She was so clever – she knew so much about so much – but she wouldn't have me. I was young. And I couldn't be in a relationship without power anyway. And Mo was such a prick sometimes – you know, the other day, like last week – literally last week, this time – he came into my room and asked me which headshot looked better on newsprint. What was weird was that he didn't come to my room to watch games or eat Tostitos now. It was still football season.

"I really have to be getting back to my group," I said.

"Oh," she said, her eyebrows raised. "Who are you with?"

"No one…That you know… A guy…from the Jewish Center."

"I see."

I could not find Aliza. Not in front of the Toulouse-Lautrec or the Henri Rousseau. I got nervous. Then I heard voices from the next gallery.

"Just tell me already – w

"Mo! How many times d answer?"

I turned. The male's voice female's, but that she was Rosie Rosie – I had no doubt. So they Who had orchestrated this – George

"Look," said Mo. "I won't take won't. I just want to know – for my o improve – who is the better writer."

Rosie sighed.

"No. You answer me. Where were y didn't respond to any of my texts."

I had to find Aliza.

I rushed out of the 19th–century rooms.

"There you are!" she said. She was stand Picasso. "What took so long?"

"Same as last time," I said. It was a lie. I was offi IBS as my get-out-of-jail free card. This is what it down to. She was too nice to upset – far too nice.

"I wanna show you something," she said.

This time she did hail the cab. We were back in her r There was something big and rectangular – no joke – wrap up and standing against her closet.

"Open it," she said.

I clawed at the paper.

It was my first column, framed.

"You're amazing," I said, because she had put into wood and glass the sense of recognition – yes, I exist, I do those 750 words every week, why the fuck don't you read them? anyone? Out there? – I was seeking.

Nov. 25, 2005

It was a meat night so the Jewish Center cafeteria was already crowded when I got there with Mo and Vern, who had been hanging in my room for the previous 15 minutes, watching my television and reading.

"C'mon, hurry up," Mo said.

"Hold on, hold on," I said. I was trying to put the finishing touches on a column I was preparing in order to best the very person now impatiently calling. This was a push-pull. I had been meaning to ask him what I should think about Aliza and that mysterious other guy she kissed. But I didn't.

You don't reveal your longing like that, said one side of me. Said the other, He's supposed to be your friend, isn't he? If you don't ask him, who do you ask?

"Mo, Mo – listen to this," Vern said. Mo, standing in the doorway, looked down the hall toward the main door. He was practically out of the room. "Hurry – I'm hungry."

Vern read a passage from *Leviathan*: "'Not every thought to thought succeeds indifferently. But as we have no imagination whereof we have not formerly had sense, in whole, or in parts; so we have no transition from one imagination to another, whereof we never had the like before in our senses.' Isn't that amazing?"

"You're out of your mind," Mo said. But I love you."

"Okay, done," I said. I closed the laptop.

"It took you long enough," Mo said.

****

By the way, Rosie and Mo were dating by this point. And Shani was practically with Vern. I dunno that they actually were, but she loved putting her hand on his leg under the table at meals. And this was at the Jewish Center – which, as I said, gets really crowded on meat nights. Aliza and I usually sat at the far ends of our group. I'd see where she was and take the other side.

"Damn it, J! Didn't I tell you it'd be crowded?"

"Alright, alright," I said. "It's not like you're starving."

"How do you know? Maybe I have an intestinal parasite – ever thought of that?"

By the way, Mo is living with me next semester. My roommate decided to go back to Israel and study. So this guy and his parasite are moving in.

And then the girls walked in. Rosie went over to Mo. Shani found Vern. That left us. We were all standing on line for cold-cut wraps.

"Hi," I said.

"Hi," she said.

"About what I told you, at the museum…"

"No, don't…"

"No, I should. I didn't hook up with anyone."

I was stunned. It was like time had been reversed – to paraphrase George Costanza, it was like having Superman spin the Earth backwards in time.

"You didn't?"

"No."

"Then, what about....?"

"I know this is gonna sound ridiculous. Please don't hold it against me."

I would never.

"I would never."

The blood was rushing to my cheeks.

"Good. I said it because I needed to know. For sure. That you cared."

"You what?"

"I know. It was stupid. I told you not to hold it against me."

"No – no!" That was the last thing I wanted her to think. "I'm not holding anything but this red tray. Honest."

"And I knew it was stupid and I saw your reaction and I should've just ended it there. But then, once I had said it, I didn't want you to think I was a liar, so I kept quiet."

I didn't know what to say. But I was thrilled.

"Do you wanna get out of here?"

She looked at me like I was kidding.

"What about dinner?"

"I'll make you a grilled cheese in my room. C'mon."

She smiled and we dropped our trays by the salad bar and left the room. I could almost hear Mo say something about it behind my back.

****

"This is hot and gooey."

She was right, the cheese was dripping from the bread. I handed her some tin foil and we wrapped them up.

"Where are you taking me?" she asked. "I thought we were gonna eat here."

I had an idea.

****

"This is perfect." She looked out onto the water. Our feet were dangling over the river and the cheese was dangling from our mouths.

I had calculated right. Water + sandwiches = romance.

"I thought you'd like it."

We ate. I sneaked peeks at her. Her neck and face was covered in shadow. There was a streetlight above us; the parts of her it kept bright were enough – the end of her nose, the brown glint in her eyes. Long reddish-brown hair.

I leaned in. She pulled back.

"What are you doing?"

What did she think I was doing?

"Trying to kiss you."

"Oh."

She stayed still. I moved in again. Our lips met.

This is fucking awesome, I thought. Her tongue tasted like soggy Cheerios. I was kissing the girl I wanted. I put my hands around her waist, on her back, on the back of her head – in her hair. She made little sounds – peeps and gasps. I gripped her leg. I felt finally connected to her. I didn't feel there was anything more we could do to be closer. If we had sex then – and obviously that wasn't happening – I still don't think I could've felt closer to her. It just happened, was natural – that feeling. I didn't need to do anything.

"I really like you," I said. It was a break and we were breathing. You could see our breaths on the water. She had on this big smile. And then she didn't.

She pulled away.

"There's something you should know."

Shit.

"Did you actually hook up with that guy?"

"No. There is no guy. I'm dying."

"What?" I felt my body go cold.

"I'm dying." She sounded flat – as if she had already come to grips with it. Was she serious?

"Are you serious?"

"Yeah, I'm dying."

"How can you sound so calm? And what do you have?"

"I have a fine arts class. You know that. We're working with inks. Dying."

She broke into a grin, slowly.

I was stunned. That fucking prankster! My heart was racing.

"I cannot believe you did that." She would continue to exist. She would be a real thing.

"I'm sorry. I know that was evil." She laughed. "I got you pretty good, though."

"You can't keep doing this – toying with my emotions."

"I know."

"Don't get me wrong. I'm really glad you're gonna be around."

"Me, too."

I kissed her – on the cheek. Then the lips. She put her head on my shoulder.

"You're a ridiculous prankster," I said.

"Would it have changed things?" she whispered.

Jan. 17, 2006

The door opened with a squeak.

"Boy, it's dark in here."

Mo and I were entering the room after Friday night dinner at the Jewish Center. He didn't go into his room – he went into mine. Which presented this weird thrill. He hadn't been in my room in awhile – since the end of the regular football season.

"You looking to sleep with me tonight?"

Why was I discouraging him?

No answer.

"Is this in honor of Shabbos? It's Friday night, so we're gonna do something special and switch rooms?"

More discouragement (was that a word?).

"You make it seem so unusual for me to be in here. I *am* your roommate."

"You rarely venture down the hall."

"Maybe I want to talk tonight."

He rolled onto my bed.

I rolled the chair closer. I was excited.

"'Bout what?"

"College?"

"Okay."

"You first."

I didn't know what he wanted me to say. Didn't want to lose the opportunity either.

"Are you serious?"

"Do I sound it?"

"You're putting me on the spot here."

"Take your time."

The room was dead quiet. A few feet away from us was the dark window. It looked like a sheet had been draped over it, it was so dark.

The words just came from me:

"It is as beautiful to me as a deep, black night."

"Huh?"

"It's a line from 'Avalon Landing.'"

"Never got around to reading it...Also, I'm waiting."

He turned over, so that his eyes were on the ceiling. College? What could I say? It was important that I say something. Stories about things would make us close.

"Alright...So when I imagined college as a boy, it was always in one of two ways."

"If you say so."

"Either it was like the fraternity in 'Animal House,' or else it was like one giant slumber party with friends and late-night secrets and cozy sleeping bags and endless cookies."

"That sounds nice."

"Except none of my sleepover parties ever turned out that way —they all wound up sucking. You know what it's like...you have a long day of basketball and your eyes hurt and you tuck yourself into the sleeping bag and try to nod off and every time you do you're knocked by a boy falling off the couch above you, trying to catch a ball in a game of flies-up."

"I have no idea what that's like. I was always the kid who could fall asleep."

The bastard.

"I hate you. I always had to tell them to stop, but they kept falling, and eventually that became the object of the game — who could fall on me."

I saw his head move up and down on the pillow. Then it appeared his eyes were closed. Good sign? Or was I boring?

"Once they had noticed how bothered you were, that became the game's goal. And they'd purposely throw the ball wide or purposely leap off the couch. And one time, they landed on my nose, and it felt totally smushed. And of course I started crying. And I tried to hide it by looking away but someone yelled, 'He's a crybaby!' And I felt really angry, like I had to do something. So there was this kid – Sivan – who was obviously the weakest one. He was at this sleepover, and he was the only other one *not* playing the game, but somehow I didn't think of that – I was so mad – and I just pushed him really hard. You should've seen his face. His ugly face. He didn't get it – at all. And I felt so guilty."

I sighed. There was sweat on my forehead. Mo raised his arms above his shoulders, as if about to yawn. I was trying to keep it engaging.

"It's fucking hard being a little boy," he said.

"You get it." I hadn't meant to say that aloud.

"Of course I get it. I am the one who came in here and laid down on your bed."

"I guess you are."

"Continue."

"It wasn't just that I had picked on the kid who was easiest to pick on. Sivan looked like a dweeb, but we all did. I was mad at myself because I was more observant than other kids, so I should've been the last guy to push Sivan. I had seen the signs from the first grade. He was poor. He always wore clunky Airwalks, never Nikes, and his clothes were faded hand-me-downs – old flannel shirts and—"

"I get it. You don't have to beat yourself up."

"Okay."

"Back to the sleepovers. Because you got off-track."

He was definitely ordering me.

"I did have a few good ones — not at parties, but with one or two other guys, either at their house or mine…Most of them were with Avi. He's the guy who first told me about bands – Boyz II Men, the Backstreet Boys. I didn't know what pop music was."

"Smart kid, you were…"

"One night I was lying on the top bunk and I heard a thud, so I crawled to the side-rail and looked down and Avi was trying to maneuver his way out of the bed without waking me. He saw me and said, 'I gotta run downstairs and check something.' A few minutes later he came in with this grin on his face. I said, 'Avi, what's going on?' And he said to me that he had checked the TV guide and a porno was coming on at 12:30 and would I come down and watch. And I remember – I'll never forget – my cheeks got so flushed. I felt this acid or whatever in my stomach and I said, 'I dunno…I'll see when the time comes,' even though I wanted to go…"

"Did you?" He had risen in the bed. He was eager.

"Naw…I chickened out."

"Aww, Jeremiah. You suck."

"I know."

"I feel like you missed out on a big part of childhood." He laughed. "Like isn't that how all kids learn how to jack off – at sleepover parties?"

"I always thought it was summer camp."

"That, too."

"I did, actually, learn at a sleepover party."

"No shit…"

"Yeah, it was awkward. Thinking about it now, I can't even tell you."

"No, please do." A request.

"I had this friend with a bunch of older brothers. We'll call him David. One Friday night, me and Matthew and the other Matthew were sleeping on the floor in his basement, 'cause that's where he used to put us. David asked whether we knew how to do it. I don't even know whether that was word he used – 'it,' I mean, I can't remember whether we knew the word 'masturbation.' He said, 'I'm gonna show you,' and he had older brothers, so we listened. He pulled his hand out from his pocket– his right hand – and he basically spread his index finger from his pointer – like he was making the peace sign and—"

"What the hell was this – some kind of anti-Vietnam protest jerk-off?"

"Very funny, Mr. I'm-Gonna-Lie-on-Someone-Else's-Bed-and-Force-Him-to-Divulge-Stories-Without-Sharing-Jackshit-in-Return?"

I was trying to show him I was tough. That I didn't feel I needed to tell him things.

"I'll share something when you're done. Honest." I believed him.

"David made the peace sign and took two outstretched fingers and lowered them into his pants and knocked it around. I didn't know what the hell was going on. He wasn't jerking it, though. Just getting it hard. I stood there watching. That that must've lasted a few minutes. I can't imagine he was able to get hard really quickly in front of a bunch of guys – but who the hell knows? In retrospect, it's such a fucked-up story I guess anything's possible."

Mo brushed a hair out of his eye.

"After a few minutes of playing pinball with himself he went into the bathroom. Now, mind you, I had no idea exactly what he did in there — I had just heard him say something about Vaseline when he went in and the word 'fantastic' when he went out...."

"Jesus."

I looked down at my hands, which were positioned on my lap. They seemed to be in the wrong place but I couldn't figure a better one to place them. My cheeks were hot.

"Alright...Enough of me. How about you?"

Mo sat up.

"How about me?"

"I mean, what the hell were you like back?"

"In sixth grade?"

"Yeah...or whenever."

"Well..." Mo slunk down, into the bed, and turned to the wall, away from me. "There was this girl..."

"OOOOH – a girl. Already this is good."

"Uhright, uhright – calm down, Romeo...Yes, there was a girl. Her name was Tali."

"TA-LI! Gotta love that name. Just goes perfect in sports chants. Here we go Ta-li, here we go!"

"Do you want me to tell this story or not? 'Cause if not, we can just end it here, without my having to listen to your cheering..."

"No, no – continue."

"Okay, good. So...Tali...She was older. *Forceful*...She's not that different from Caroline."

"Can it."

"Anyway, that's not important. What's important is Tali. She wore glasses and pigtails and took lessons in opera singing. I'm not kidding about that, by the way. She went to some teacher – from the age of 6 – to learn how to use her lungs. I remember, she used to walk up to me – right? – and she'd just puff out her chest and open her mouth wide and start going, 'AAAAAAH.' And I guess it was all innocent when she was 6, but you gotta remember, by the time I was in sixth grade, she was already in eighth. She had breasts."

"So it's come to this, then – eighth-grader breasts?"

"Sure. Anyway, she was very outspoken about what was right, right? And I remember, on the bus ride home – 'cause she was on my bus – I mean, we actually got off at the same stop, this little cul-de-sac in front of the Katz's house – anyway, on the way home, she was always bossing the little kids around – telling them that their handwriting was bad or their plaid shirts were ugly – things like that."

"Sounds like you were whipped."

"Yeah – exactly – we all were whipped. And I mean, even though I was in sixth grade, and even though she already had hooters, I still didn't think of her as more than the bossy girl who appointed herself bus monitor. But then, one day, we're getting off the bus, right in front of the Katzs', and she kinda looks at me – before I can even turn toward my place, which I used to reach by cutting through a backyard – and says, '*Come.*'"

"Intimidating."

"Yeah. So of course, I followed. We walked down the street – straight into the Steins' backyard. They were this crabby old couple who had a kid who'd died in a car crash. And they scared me. So I was doubly afraid. Number one, I was scared of this bossy girl whose orders I had to follow and two, I was scared of the people whose property I was trespassing."

"I'd be scared, too." Empathy: the whole point to sharing stories. I was giving it up.

"Yeah – and I was as far from being a bad boy as you can be. But that day, I dunno, I felt I had to listen."

"Sure."

"Anyway, she led us to this dark area beneath the Steins' porch. There was a garden hose there, in the dirt. I still remember – it was hooked up to the little faucet. She said, 'Stand here,' so I stepped onto the hose and then she positioned herself so she was facing me and she looked up at me – for like a split-second, not even enough time for me to really slow down and figure out what was going on. She grabbed my hand, and I remember thinking, 'Oh, god – where is she gonna put this thing?'"

"You said that?"

"No – but I was thinking it. So anyway, she said, 'I want you to feel something,' and she dragged my hand over her hips."

"What?!"

"I know. First one side, then the other. And not fast either, J. *Slow.* Like a caress."

Mo sat up on the bed, and I saw the redness in his cheeks. He pushed himself off with both hands and shuffled toward me – his eyes focused downward, on the carpet.

"My throat's dry."

He went to the sink and grabbed a plastic cup he kept by the mirror and filled it. Sitting in my seat, I could hear him gulp it all down. I was excited. I was trying to think of the tale I would tell next – because it seemed we were taking turns.

Then, from the hallway:

"I think I'll turn in."

No!

"Now?"

"Yeah."

A few footsteps, and then the yawn of his old bedroom door. I shook my head and got up. I looked around. My sheets were all mussed and the PJs that had been spread upon them were on the floor. I picked them up and changed.

I slid into bed, but my face felt hot, so I peeled off the sheets and lay bare. I thought I could hear my heart in my head. Minutes passed.

Rap-rap.

I turned over, to the wall the sound had come from. I placed my ear against it. Silence. And then, a few seconds later:

Rap-rap.

Mo, I realized – it must be Mo knocking for me – letting me know he was still awake. He also couldn't sleep. These were not words. But neither are African drumbeats. It counted.

Slowly I balled my right hand into a fist and raised it against the wall. I rapped it. felt my pulse quicken. I took a deep breath and pulled the hand back toward my chest. Then, after a pause, I let it swing again.

I waited and looked out on the room on my other side: the green-faced alarm clock, the plastic filing cabinet, the bags of granola and the folded newspapers on my bookshelves – the columns I had saved. This place was so filled with me – all my stuff and compositions. And Mo's room was probably the same. But there were volleys between them – sounds echoing from one to another.

I watched a tree through the window. It was blown by the wind and it scraped up against the building a bit. Some branches looked like they might fall. And there was a howling noise. And then:

Rap-Rap.

March 26, 2006

We joined clubs. Aliza did a fashion thing. Rosie did microlending and became a newspaper copy-editor. Shani launched her own student gossip magazine.

Vern was offered a position in the secretive student literary club — the Zelosophic Society. I dunno why this matters. I think because it leaves me and Mo to our writing. I could always find him in his room, scraping his fingers along the keys. His back was bent, like the end of a hanger, his body heavy like a bag of sand. And always, his eyes were squinted, as if trying to expel a dried-up lens. I looked at him through a crack in the door. He never acknowledged me, though I didn't think he was being mean. Just busy.

Meanwhile, I spent all my time writing. If he had visited, though, I would've said, 'Hi,' and tried to draw him out. There had been no more storytelling, and I asked him to room with me (again) the next year.

****

The banquet hall seemed to press down on its occupants, like the top of a griddle or a low-pitched tent.

We met in my apartment to pregame. I was there, of course, because of my column, but all my friends had there reasons. Rosie was invited to the newspaper banquet because she was a copy-editor; Shani because her TV segment was featured in a recent article; Vern was invited because he was dating Shani — as Aliza was for dating me; and Mo had been asked to speak about being a rogue journalist because his column had been rejected by the paper but was now more widely read than it.

I thought to myself. That's a lot of bullshit. The only thing rogue is the way he doesn't return my comments.

There two other speakers – the school president, who tried to make fun of the newspaper because it spent the year making fun of her; and the outgoing editor-in-chief, whose job it was to present the annual awards (for best reporting, best feature writing, best in office whiskey-sipping).

My room was once again packed with friends. The heater blew a dry heat, and the desk was strewn with bottles and cups. People lounged on the chairs, on the bed and on the floor, though Mo, rehearsing his remarks, kept pacing up and down the hall, muttering to himself.

The pregame conversation focused on the literary society.

"What do you do up there?" we kept asking, and Vern, no more or less calm than usual, kept shrugging.

"I bet it's a secret cache of porno," said Shani.

"Yeah, that makes *perfect* sense," said Aliza.

She was sitting on my bed, a Solo cup in her hands, playing with the edge of her black dress. It was a striking, silky piece – hung off the shoulders – almost '80s style – and cut deep over the breasts in a perfect V – a letter with which I already associated all femininity.

When you look at a girl you're dating – whom you may love – at a party and no one else is, and then she turns her head up and smiles, you feel you two share a secret – a delightful secret.

"Whatever they do, it's clearly not important," Rosie said. She bared her Chiclet-white teeth imperiously, then hastened once again to hide them. "I mean, you don't ever see them sponsor campus events, *do* you? It's not like they get anything *done.*"

Vern shrugged.

"You're sober – that's the problem," said Mo, who over my desk was now pouring out flavored vodka. "Take this. You'll be more agreeable."

Rosie downed it.

It was not long before we were giddily marching down the Alley, to the on-campus hotel at Ash and 36th. The night had a kind of final darkness to it. Already, the weather had turned temperate and spring-like in the days, and only the nights now remained to remind us of the winter.

Aliza gripped my hand.

Off the lobby, we climbed a staircase to reach the hors d'oeuvres and open bar (which, combined with the three-course meal, and banquet hall rental, was said to cost $26,500 – a figure about commensurate to the collective drunkenness). The doors to the ballroom were closed.

"Let's get trashed," said Vern.

"Are you serious?" I asked. "What happened to Schopenhauer and pessimism?"

He laughed.

"That has its place. But I'm not unwilling to have fun."

Vern ordered a drink at the bar. Mo slapped my back.

"I guess that leaves you and me."

I wondered whether I should ask him about the contract. I decided against.

"Let's have a drink," I said.

We stepped up to the bar to order. Vern was at the other end, talking to someone. We got screwdrivers.

****

The speeches were mercifully short – except Mo's. Then there was dancing. By my fifth, I was feeling pretty loose.

Aliza click-clacked her shiny heels against the tiles, dipped her hips and, in the same motion, ran her right hand up through her long hair, pushing it back. That was her move. I've always imagined her naked with that hair, with her breasts obscured only by long flowing locks, like Alanis Morissette's, just without the edginess. I cannot dance quite as well, but under the influence, I shuffled on my tippy-toes like a boxer and earnestly claimed they so danced in the chicest clubs of downtown Manhattan. Had you asked me, obviously, I would have been unable either to name a club or locate the area intended by "downtown," but it didn't matter. We kept moving, rubbing against each other, and we got hot and red-faced. It was hard work, too, continuing on song after song, and I felt a burn run up my calves, especially when I wrapped Aliza from behind to grind. I had to spread my legs wide, to lower my height and make it work, and by the end, it was all I could do just to balance. I kept walking over to the bar, grabbing a few cocktail chips, filmed in that reddish nacho-cheese powder, and wiping my brow with the small square napkins.

"I need a break," Vern said at one point. He and Shani were dancing next to us. So were Mo and Rosie.

"You're here as *my* escort," Shani said. "You can't bail."

"I know, but..."

"Let's get beers," Mo said to me, nodding toward the bar.

We were at the edge of the carpet. Behind us, the tangled bodies were like an upside down spider. I looked at Aliza, for permission. She nodded okay.

"Do you want anything?"

She didn't. Mo and I walked toward the bar, I remembered the paper in my jacket pocket.

"Two Coronas," he said.

"Mo," I said, tapping him on the shoulder. "I have the contract."

"What?"

"Here."

I took it out and unfolded it.

He bent over. I don't think he knew what I was talking about. But then he saw the words and he rose up from the paper.

"I can't sign this, Jeremiah."

I thought we had agreed. He hadn't gotten around to signing it – true – and I had taken to carrying the paper with me at all times to get him to – also true – but he had never objected to the idea.

"Why?"

"*Because.*"

"Because what?"

"I think it'll ruin the friendship if we live together again. We'll always have to talk to each other."

"Isn't that what friends do?" I was totally baffled.

"Yeah, but it can get excessive. Like if I have to ask you everyday what you ate that day, you'll begin to resent it, and so will I."

That shit sounded like a weak excuse. I felt there was something else. How could I not?

"If you say so."

****

The DJ made an announcement. There would be a swing dance contest.

"Jeremiah – there you are!"

It was Aliza. She had slithered out of the crowd.

"I was looking for you."

"I was looking for *you*."

"Can we join the contest?"

"Yes."

She took me by the hand and led me to the middle of the floor. Already standing there were Rosie and Mo and Shani.

"Where's Vern?" I asked.

"I don't know," Shani said. She sounded pissed.

Soon it was on.

The music began slowly, which was good – as I had never really danced in my life. I learned very quickly that Mo had. Actually, he had taken lessons in high school. It had been a senior year alternative to phys-ed. He was good. And Rosie, though usually first in everything, followed his lead.

Aliza and I had much more difficulty. I kept glancing over to our competitors, to copy their moves, but by the time I had returned to my own partnership, I was behind.

Meanwhile, around us, as one song gave way to the next, couples were dropping out. The DJ went around tapping shoulders, almost indiscriminately. The guys always had the same look – the one whose outward meaning was "Now, surely you've made some mistake" and whose inner meaning was – "Look, man. You know what it's like to try and impress a girl. Give me a break."

I kept expecting a hand to pat me, but none came. We were the final couple with Rosie and Mo.

"Each couple will have 30 seconds," said the DJ.

They went first. They did all the things you see in movies. Like it was the Savoy Ballroom or something. Their finishing move was one to behold. Mo flung Rosie outward, and she spun back into his arms. Then he hoisted her up and swung her between his legs. And she flew into the air and landed on his shoulders.

When the music started for us, I was frozen. Aliza stared at me – she was embarrassed. Finally, she grabbed *my* hand and pulled me into the middle of the floor. She spun, dipped and twirled me. Around and around we went. We were like amusement park teacups. I gained confidence. I decided I'd try to throw her up in the air at the end and copy Mo.

The toss part I did okay. But to be honest, her weight was awkwardly distributed in her body (I dunno where it was, but it wasn't in her bottom like I thought it would be). And when she landed on me I wobbled. My knees buckled. And I fell.

The crowd gasped.

I was looking up. Aliza was lying near me, her hands on her ribs. Shani was above us.

"Are you okay?" she asked.

"I think so," said Aliza. She glared at me.

They helped her off. I was left there, unassisted. Rosie and Mo were announced as the winners. I crawled through the crowd to reach the carpet at the end of the dance floor.

"Tough break," I heard a man's voice say. I looked up, my chin deep in the carpet's pile. I could make out a chair and a table and tufts of white hair, and ruddy cheeks. A thin white beard, triangular, like a bowling alley's lacquered arrows, became visible. A head was bending down.

It was Hutchinson.

"I like your writing," he said. He offered me a hand. I grasped it. "It's good."

He paused.

"Only don't use so many words. You need to be more confident."

****

Aliza and I hobbled down the Alley in a pack of about 10. The after-party was at an off-campus house five blocks away, and it seemed to us that we were swimming. It felt like 10 minutes just to go one block. I had my arm draped over her shoulders, and she had hers around my waist. My shirt was untucked, and the cool air pressed against my back.

Walking into such a party was like walking into a bar. The Smirnoff air hinted at what was going on in the basement.

We walked down the stairs. It was hazy from the pot and there wasn't much light. But we could see a bit. A varsity basketball player was surrounded by four girls half his height. They peered up at him from his waist, and he looked down googly eyed, his head drooping forward. He looked like a tree about to fall. Actually, in the corner, a columnist did just that. He was reclining on a La-Z-Boy. He leaned over the plush arm like someone on a boat and puked.

"You wanna get out of here?" I asked her. She nodded. We climbed back up and wandered the hallways.

"Here," I said. We walked into an empty bedroom. I shut the door behind us as she crawled into the bed.

"Spoon with me," she said. It sounded like something I had heard before. I got in and put my arm over her arm. She clasped my hand.

"Do you remember," she said, "when I got mad because you asked about my dad and Woody Allen?"

"Yeah."

"I'm sorry about that. I had a good reason."

I really didn't care. I didn't need to know. This was all enough.

"It doesn't matter now."

"I want to tell you. It was because I lied."

Uh-oh.

"About?"

"About having a dad. I don't. He died when I was two."

"Oh."

I was startled, but not upset. She went on to say that after her father's death her mom had been distraught, how her mom never really got over it, how she neglected her kid because all she could do was grieve and how Aliza had to go live with her aunt because her mom couldn't bear the sight of her. Someone beat her during this time, but I couldn't tell from the story whether it was her mom or the aunt. She spent some time in a foster home, too.

"You don't blame me, do you?" she asked.

I didn't need to know her secrets, I thought. So no, I didn't blame her for obscuring the truth. She was already revealed to me this way – just being in my arms.

Sophomore Year

Sept. 3, 2006

My father silently sped down the New Jersey Turnpike. My mom, sitting across from him, in the front, this year, kept picking up a John Grisham paperback only to put it down. "I can't read in a car," she said. "It makes me sick."

I looked out the window.

Everything was oddly blue. The ground seemed to reflect the sky.

It was early afternoon when we arrived. My dad remained in the car, the radio tuned to a live rock concert.

"Unload your stuff," he said. "We've only got an hour."

My mom frowned and walked to the back of the car. The trunk popped open and she began placing items on the ground. I took stuff from the back seat.

"What's this?" she asked. I turned. She was holding up a big white box, inside of which was the expensive coffee-maker I had bought.

"Nothing. Just a big condom."

She shook her head.

We packed everything into a cardboard cart the school rented out and pushed up the ramp into the lobby. Matt the Security Guard was sitting there.

"Hey, Jeremiah. Long time."

"*You're* telling me."

I rolled my eyes – in my mother's direction – and he laughed.

"I'll let you get back to move-in."

My mom pressed the button and the elevator came. Mo was already inside.

"Mo!" said my mother, as she extended her hand.

He shook it.

I felt so uncomfortable. I didn't want these worlds colliding right now, to paraphrase George Costanza. And also, I didn't want my mom to ask why I wasn't living with Mo. I didn't have an answer.

A ding. The elevator doors opened. Mo walked off and said, "See you later." He sounded genuine.

Sept. 6, 2006

The freshman stared at his plastic cup in disgust.

"This tastes like urine."

His friend bent over to sniff it.

"It *is* urine."

Mo and I watched from a distance.

"This place is full of freshmen," he said.

"Yeah."

We had heard a big party was gonna go down here. It was the night before classes were to start. But this was it. And the girls and Vern hadn't come yet.

We shook our heads and looked around. It was a longish, white-walled room that had been emptied of furniture (and where instead there were now two long rectangular tables filled with boxes of Franzia wine and six-packs of Lionshead). A lot of the kids had on bracelets and necklaces with wooden beads.

Mo went to the table and grabbed us beers. Handing me mine, he appeared to linger there – in my grip. I thought if I held I'd be letting him have his way. And if he didn't want to live with me, I wasn't going to let him stay in my hand whenever he wanted. That probably makes me fucking crazy, but I saw a connection – or felt one.

The music came from the other room. It was a cover band.

She was just 17

You know what I mean

Mo spotted two empty chairs against the wall and we decided to sit. The music got louder and so, too, the sound of feet being stamped.

I'll never dance with another…whoo!

When I saw her standing there

The girls finally arrived, Vern in-tow.

"Where'd you find him?" Mo asked.

"He was outside on the front steps," Shani said, "reading."

Aliza came right up to me and hugged me.

"I missed you," I said. I hadn't seen her for the last few weeks. She had been on vacation with her family in Turkey.

"I missed you, too." Her hair was as reddish as ever and her skin as dark. It was that Middle-Eastern sun.

Rosie took a few steps into the room and surveyed it.

"We can't stay here. There's no one our age."

Mo nodded. They were also kind of snuggling now. Except his arms were barely around her – like he was afraid of catching something.

A scene played out before us. We all watched, but Shani seemed especially interested.

"But last night?" a girl sighed.

The boy looked away, then kicked his shoe against the floor.

"Just a hook-up...That's all."

The girl's eyes widened.

"What?!"

"You heard me."

Just then, another girl – a blonde – approached from the darkness. She was short and curvy and her eyes were peppermint green.

"Will you come to my party later?"

I smiled.

"That's sweet of you, but we don't hang out with freshmen."

She rolled her eyes.

"I wasn't talking to *you*."

She bent down to Vern's level, lifting his chin with her hand.

"Listen, cutie. Birthday House 315. At 1-ish. I expect to see you there."

She blew him a kiss and walked away.

Vern and I gawked.

****

We wound up in a Southern fraternity.

Mo grinded with an unfamiliar girl. She was Indian – dark and short with straightened hair and wide, black eyes.

"What's he up to?" I asked Vern, but Vern didn't have an answer. He had also brought a book about the history of rivers, which he was reading. Aliza pulled me to the table where the drinks were. I think we were both shocked by all the energy drinks.

"Someone's gonna have a heart attack," I said. She agreed. They were pretty intimidating, the cans, too – some of them had skulls and tattoo-like images and there was Red Bull, of course, and Monster and Rockstar.

Aliza seemed to be in a wandering mood so I followed her around the house. "Have you ever been here before?" I asked. She said no, but she wanted to take a look for herself.

We climbed the stairs to the second floor. At the end a door was open. "Let's go in," she said. I followed her and then we were at some guy's desk and there was a felt dart board on the wall.

"Punch the target," she said.

"No way." The wall seemed pretty hard, even with the covering. And I didn't see much of a reason for me to be hitting things.

"How drunk are you?" I asked.

"I'm not." She sounded offended by the implication.

I said, Ok, in that case, she was being weirdly violent. She wrapped her arms around me and looked up in my eyes and said if I loved her, I would punch the wall. I told her if I loved her I would keep my hands nice and uninjured so I could caress her without being in terrible freaking pain. It was supposed to get a laugh – I was trying to make a weird situation funny – 'cause I had no idea what was going on and laughs are a good way to get around that. But she was very serious.

"If you really love me, you'll do it," she said. Then I think she saw the fear in my eyes – because it was hard to hide. "I know it sounds crazy. But I've been through a lot in my life – when I was growing up – and I need this. It's something I need to see. So do it, please. For me."

What the hell? I thought. This seems crazy to me – and more than that, unnecessary – like I don't need this to show anything. But it wouldn't hurt that much. And she wanted it. And the look on her face – the puppy-dog eyes and the imploring lips – told me it meant something greater, that I couldn't understand.

I wound up and threw a right hand.

The pain was intense. And throbbing.

****

I was back downstairs, talking to Shani. I held my one fist in my other. The space between my knuckles had puffed up so it was like I was wearing a purple band around my hand.

"She needs to stop," Shani said. She pointed to Rosie.

"Stop what?"

"That's her third Red Bull."

"No way. She'd be dead."

"I'm telling you. I've been watching."

That's no good, I thought. I don't want one of my friends having a heart attack.

"You gotta say something," I said.

"I tried already."

Just then Vern walked up to us.

"Jelly-Maia," he said. "Shoomi."

"Geez," Shani said. "How much have you had?"

Vern lifted an empty cup.

"Jush thish."

"What was in there?"

"Bacarpi...One fifty one."

"Jesus!"

Shani extended a hand, to steady him. He stepped back and began to shake. Then he seemed to snap out of it and come to his senses.

"Gotta go!" he said. He walked past us, out of the house.

Shani and I stood silently for a moment.

"I don't get him, your boyfriend," I said.

****

We trounced through the crumpled grass, onto the Alley's stones. Rosie had had a lot to drink and a lot of energy drinks. A bad combo.

"Do you want one?" she kept asking Mo. She was referring to some pill she had in her pocket.

"No," he said.

"They want you to take a pill everyday. I mean, the doctors. The doctors don't want you to forget – to get into a bad habit. So they give you four weeks of pills, see? I mean, actually, it's not the doctors. But the drug companies. They want you to get into the habit of taking pills. That's how they make money. Good habits. You know, when I was at the UN I did a whole paper on habits. Did I tell you that already? I probably did, but I'll tell you again—"

"Please don't. I remember."

"Okay, another time. But I will not forget. So don't think you can get out of it. Because you can't. My brain is speedy. I remember all. Like Stephen Hawking, or Ayn Rand."

Mo shook his head. We were heading to the Quad – to that party Vern had been invited to (even though Vern wasn't with us). We passed the Benjamin Franklin statue and light posts and lecture halls. They were all shadowed and dark. But there was a light coming from the top of one of the buildings.

"It's in the lit society," Shani said. "The Zelosophic Club, or whatever it's called."

Mo peered upward.

"It looks like a guy bent over a desk," he said.

****

We were in a bedroom in the Quad.

"It's no big deal," said a boy to Aliza.

"It *is* a big deal," she said. "You were a ranked tennis player."

"Only as a junior."

"Only as a junior! Who cares? You played in the U.S. Open!"

"It's true," I said. I wanted to get myself in this conversation somehow – I didn't like Aliza talking to just one other guy. "Being in the U.S. Open is a huge deal. She's right."

Aliza tucked a hand into the back pocket of my jeans. We walked into the hallway. "Let's explore," she said.

"You're really in a mood," I said. I meant it like she kept wanting to go places and do things but it came out wrong.

Anyway we wound our way down the hall into a lounge. There was a computer sitting on one of the tables.

"Take it," she said. I was shocked and flabbergasted. What? Was she insane? She wanted me to steal a fucking laptop? But then, I hadn't understood the target thing either and I was pretty sure I was beginning to perceive just how deep an impact her childhood had had on her. So I wasn't mean or loud – just calm.

"I don't think that's a good idea."

She huffed. "I didn't say anything about it being a good idea. I just want you to do it."

I stepped away from her, back toward the hallway.

"Aliza," I said. "I love you. You know that. But I can't steal someone's laptop." Which was about exactly what I was feeling – though the conflict inside of me was deeper. Not about whether I should do it. I would've never done it. But about whether I could really love a girl I was finding out was a bit unhinged.

She moved close to me.

"We're sophomores now," she said. I was with her so far. "And I know you say you love me but we've been together for awhile. And I need something more."

"I'll do anything," I said. "But this is wrong."

"That's why I need you to do it. If it weren't—"

"I can't. I just can't."

"Just show me." She put her hands around my neck. "Please show me."

I backed away, into the hall.

"No."

She turned her back on me and I heard her cry. I ran off.

Sept. 7, 2006

I sat alone in the middle of the 500-seat lecture hall. It was all red —the walls, the carpet, the cloth-padded chairs. Soon it was filled with Greek History students

"Welcome back to school, folks."

The professor looked out on us.

"Look, I don't want to be awake right now either. Or here, for that matter. Do you know I was actually asked out on a brunch date this morning?"

We laughed.

"It's true. Another professor – a woman named Scots – do you know her? – asked me. And I was about to say yes, when I remembered this stupid class."

We laughed more.

"Anyway, I'm saying this to let you know I'm also sacrificing. I don't need to be here. I don't need an intro course. I know the material."

He paused.

"You. You tell me why we're studying the Greeks."

He pointed to a boy.

"Um…"

During all of this I was on my computer IMing Shani. She was half a campus away in math lecture. I told her what Aliza had tried to make me do and she responded with astonishment – but I could tell it was faked. Aliza had gotten to her first and told her her side of things, which I couldn't even imagine.

Then she told me: "Mo broke it off with Rosie last night."

I told her I didn't believe it and she said, "I think he cheated." I said no way and she said, "Just wait. You'll see."

Everyone around me suddenly rose from his seat. As one the students dragged their bags from the floor onto their hunched backs. A voice went up from the podium below but was practically drowned out.

"And don't forget – chapter one in the textbook! For tomorrow! Don't forget!"

Half the class was already outside. The professor's head drooped onto his chest. He looked like a wilted flower or recently-engorged labia majora from which blood flees. "TTYL" I typed. And, snapping the Dell closed, I stuffed it in my bag and shuffled to the door.

Dec. 1, 2006

The group could hardly still be called one. Rosie became the head of her microfinance club and ran for the treasurer position with her prestigious all-girl a cappella group – the Clef Palettes. Incidentally, all her running around and coffee-drinking made her ragged but in a beautiful way. A Kate Moss way.

Shani spent all her time on this gossip magazine she had started. It was pretty good, I had to admit. All glossy and filled with juicy stuff about kids I knew. My fear was that I'd become a part of it somehow – everyone's fear. She had this feature – Shoutouts – they were anonymous student submissions directed toward other students and everyone knew what they meant and whom they targeted. Here's an example:

To the Orthodox Girl Whose Oral Sex Blows,
Since when is cocaine kosher?
Love,
Your Still-Passionate ex-Goyfriend.

The student council threatened to pull funding for her magazine because of this feature. There was a trial coming up about the issue.

Vern spent his time in the lit society and Mo and I wrote. Aliza I still saw every night – even though her fashion club was putting together a runway show – but things were different between us. Since the laptop thing, I had been afraid of saying or doing anything that would trigger the weird side of her. She was a lot more quiet for her part. We still made out all the time and she let me feel her up. I couldn't get much more than that, but for a girl who had been *shomeret* at the start of school, it wasn't bad.

The whole group only got together on Friday nights.

****

I walked into the Orthodox minyan,[7] spotted Mo and took a seat next to him.

"Hey."

"Hey."

He smiled at me. The singing behind us was loud.

Heetoreri, heetoreri, ki va orech, kumi ori
Uri, uri, shir daberi, k'vod Hashem, alayich niglah![8]

Mo clapped and so did I. Vern walked in while everyone was bowing.

"That was awkward," he said, when he took a seat. We agreed.

Soon we were all downstairs in the Jewish Center lobby. Everyone could be seen. The darkness of the outside world pressed against the windows.

"Hey."

It was Aliza. She was in a slinky black dress with an empire waist.

"You look so beautiful."

I looked around, made sure no one was watching (but everyone could see me, of course – I was tall) and kissed her forehead.

"Thanks," she said.

She led me by the hand away, upstairs – back into the *minyan* room. "What are we doing up here?" I asked.

She smiled – slyly – like there was some big secret. Then she walked over to the *aron*[9] and pulled something out. It was

---

[7] Technically, this means the quorum of 10 men required for prayer in Orthodox circles but Jeremiah uses the term here to denote the synagogue.
[8] This is part of the Friday night *L'cha Dodi* song, which is sung to welcome the Sabbath Queen.
[9] The ark where the Torahs are kept.

small and fit in her palm and I couldn't tell what it was. Then she got closer. A pocket knife.

I didn't like the look of this at all.

"What are you doing with that?"

She grinned. It was scary-looking. I was freaked. She flipped it open and extended it to me.

"Here."

I took it from her – willingly, figuring it was better for me to have it anyway, no matter what she wanted me to do.

"Good." She sounded very calm. "Now I want you to slash yourself."

Oh, god. She was really fucked. This was really fucked.

"I'm not doing that." I closed the knife and thought she might advance but she merely stayed there and smiled.

"If you love me," she said, and I interrupted her.

"No – you can't pull that. This isn't funny. It's dangerous."

"I didn't say it was funny."

"It's not about love either. I don't need to do this to show you my love."

"Not a big cut." She sounded dreamy. "Just a nick."

"Do you hear yourself?"

"I'm just being honest with you." Now she sounded plaintive. "About what I need."

"If you need this," I said, "you're fucking crazy."

Tears started streaming. "Well, if that's how you feel…" She turned away. "Don't date me."

I couldn't believe this was all happening. I loved her so much.

"Fine," I said. "We're through."

****

Our arms, against the carpet, made tentacular shadows. We were in Mo's room, after dinner. It was our weekly Friday night powwow. I had told them only that Aliza and I were no longer together.

"If I saw her shit even once, I could never fuck her again."

Mo was talking about some generic girl – not about Aliza.

"But, Mo," said Vern, "just imagine the shit to be your own. When she goes in there, pretend you're the one doing it."

Mo waved his hand.

"Could never work."

"I don't know what else to tell you. You're fighting nature on this one."

Josh nodded. Josh was a *ba'al teshuva*[10].

A pause set in, in which we all slumped farther into our seats. We all drank more whiskey and the conversation turned to religion.

"If there's no God," Mo said, "it could still be worth it. If only for the wine and chicks."

Damn, he was always so easygoing. This life wasn't a place for that. He didn't need anything of it – he didn't even need God from religion.

"I disagree," I said. "These laws are too ridiculous to keep for the sake of tradition."

Josh shifted on the couch.

"Well, there *is* a god, so there's no issue."

The room went quiet. Mo grabbed for the Tropicana on the table and the plastic handle of Banker's Club. Vern poured a shot of Jack. Mo tried to get Josh to drink. Josh said no. I took the handle and poured myself.

---

[10] One who has repented his or her previous secular lifestyle and adopted Orthodoxy.

"None of you is getting the point! It's not that I'd do it for tradition," Mo said. "I'd do it for the culture."

"The culture!" I raised my voice.

"Yes, the culture."

"That's not intellectually honest."

Mo waved me off.

"Do you really think thinking things through matters? You're gonna live and die anyway. Just be blissful about it."

"It's a moot issue," Josh said, "There *is* a god."

"That's so easy for you to say." It was me. I was turning on him. Mostly because I was angry at how things turned out with Aliza.

"What are you talking about?"

"Oh, I know. You probably think it has been harder for you, because you grew up not religious and had to find God for yourself. But it's the opposite."

"You're...you're...full of shit."

"It's true. Because the rest of us, we had to go to yeshiva and listen to the teachers. About the reasons we don't eat meat and milk. Do you know how ridiculous they sound?"

"J! – lay off him," Vern said.

"Who appointed you the boss?"

Knock-knock.

The argument ceased. I felt really bad. I wanted to apologize to Josh. But there was a guy at the door – Jacob Dreyer, the puffy-yarmulke-wearing senior *ba'al teshuva* who was Josh's hero (he was also kind of my hero because I had heard that in high school he had been a huge player).

"Dreyer, my boy," said Mo. He said it in his easygoing way and slapped him on the back. "What do you say to a girl shitting? Could you take it?"

"Be a man," he said. "Suck it up."

"But it's…nasty."

"If you ignore it, you'll have the most unbelievable sex."

"Really?"

"You bet. Once she can shit in front of you, forget it. No inhibitions."

Jan. 15, 2007

"Isn't this bar great?" my date asked, pressing the circumference of the small red cocktail straw into her coated lips. We were at a frat.

"I guess," I said. "It's a bar."

"Look at the woodwork on top. They spent three months building it last year. Isn't that right, Scott?"

The bartender, in a navy sweater, nodded. Out of the corner of my eye I noticed Aliza. She was in a side room, chatting.

My date was suddenly swarmed by friends. She began telling a story.

"And then, when the teacher handed back the assignment, I said, 'Well, it didn't have these cigar ashes on the cover before!'"

Glowing with pride, she looked at her friends. They laughed. A very preppy-looking boy passed by. He had straw-colored hair that fell across his forehead like a broom. His beige corduroy pants hung just a bit short on the ankle, exposing the pale, un-socked foot in his moccasin.

"Who's Skeffington Gerard III over there?" I asked, pointing.

"Oh, that's just Chong," she said, giggling over her appletini.

"Quite the dresser, no?"

"Chong? What happened to his real parents?"

"Nothing – except for their falling in love. She was from a big steel family. His dad's Chinese."

"Oh."

"Yeah, I think they met at Brown."

Rebuked, I felt unsure of everything and decided not to speak. This was fine by my date, who briefed her short, mousy feminist friend on the "sex toy social" she had held the other night.

"I'm gonna go get another," she said, when finished. "Do you want anything?"

"No."

Aliza appeared.

"You weren't gonna say hi."

"Was I supposed to?"

"Friends *do* say hi."

"I suppose. I didn't know whether you wanted me to. I thought maybe you thought it would be awkward."

"Do *you* think it's awkward?"

The answer was yes. She could be carrying a weapon. And I loved her.

"No."

"Good. Neither do I."

"Well, it was nice talking to you."

"Always."

She went off into the room and I lost sight of her. My date had returned. She looked milky.

"Who was that?"

"An old friend."

Just then her foot slid off the side of her heel and her knee buckled and I grabbed her arm to prevent a fall. She looked up to me with a smile.

"Well, that was awfully gentlemanly of you…Want to dance?"

I nodded toward her shoes.

"Doesn't look like you're in any condition for it...not to mention the appletinis."

"Oh, *hush*. I'll cast these aside."

With that she hooked her index finger under the top strap of the stringy heels and handed them to Scott, her bartender friend. The music pulsated, but she wrapped her arms around my back and rested her head on my shoulder, as if it were a ballad. Her eyes flickered for a bit and then closed. I shuffled us toward the couches and tried to sit her down. She refused to let go of my waist.

"You're being a meanie!" she said, in the exaggerated voice of a six-year-old. "You don't want to dance with me!"

"No, no, I do...You look like you need a breather, that's all."

"Well, how about you resuscitate me?"

She leaned over with gasoline breath and hung her lips out. I met them. As her tongue, they were quite wet. Alcohol had drained no water from her.

"Yum," she said, when we were finished. She then blinked rapidly, as if bothered by a distant sight. I turned to see what it was. It was Aliza, curled up at the bottom of a staircase, crying into a nearby lap.

Jan. 18, 2007

On the line to get into the door, I eyed the bouncer, who was square as a brick, like John Cena. He inspected each entrant's ID and, depending on whether the kid was legal, gave out or denied a bracelet.

"Don't try it," said Deborah, a junior who turned had just 21. She was referring to my fake ID. "I'll get drinks for you."

I didn't answer, but instead took out my wallet and began memorizing the address and vitals.

"Don't do it," she said.

I buried my real license in the back pocket of my jeans.

"I.D.?" the bouncer asked.

"Here," I said.

"Is this you?"

"Yeah."

"No, it's not."

"It really is."

"Just go," said Deborah, pushing me forward. But I did not go.

"Look, I don't need this from you. I live at 5449 Concord Avenue, as you can see. I don't have to put up with you just because you're unable to tell."

"Go inside before I throw you out," he said, in a husky voice, laying a hand on my shoulder. "I'm keeping this."

Deborah led me in by the right hand, her lips curled into a painful grimace.

"You shouldn't have done that," she said, the words dripping with disgust.

"It was the principle."

It wasn't the principle. I was so upset about everything. Who the fuck was Deborah? Where was my girlfriend?

The place was dark and small, with an oval bar in the middle, a dance floor around that and tables against the wall.

"I need a drink," she said. We went to the bar, where she ordered a vodka tonic. I accidentally paid. She shimmied up to each of her friends and introduced me. I stared over their heads, at a nondescript point on the wall. I kept hearing "what's wrong," but got away with mouthing gibberish words in response.

I began sipping her drink, then gulping it. The bouncer, surveying the inside of the club, saw me. He approached.

"You know you can't drink."

"I *told* you – I'm 21."

"Look, put the drink down. I'll give you back the ID for 20 bucks and you won't have to leave. How about that?"

"How about that? What's wrong with you? You're forcing *me* to pay *you* to return *my* ID, which is legitimate? That's bribery! It's extortion!"

He picked me up from the elbows, clear off the ground, and carried me to a side door. He opened it, deposited me outside, and closed it with a big whoosh. The night was cold and blue. Several minutes later, Deborah poked her head out from the front door.

"I tried to convince them to let you back in. This is retarded."

"I'm sorry." Didn't mean that. I felt like the world owed me.

"What now?"

"I'll take you to another bar."

"Will you get in?"

"It can't be worse than this."

She clacked her heels onto the gum-stained pavement and we were off. The stars were out. We found ourselves in a circular booth in a neo-'50s diner-club. The teal tailfin of a fake Cadillac jutted from the wall.

"The mojitos here are so strong," she said. It sounded like: "I really want to do you, but I need to get drunk first."

The waitress walked over. She was blonde and reminiscent of Reese Witherspoon.

"What'll y'all have?"

I panicked.

"Um...tequila?"

She nodded.

"Which brand?"

"José Cuervo?"

She nodded again and walked off. I turned to Deborah. Her hand was down her dress, at work on a bra readjustment. She looked up.

"Oh, sorry. Excuse me."

This was weird but I swear I thought she was gonna pull a gun from her bra.

We were on her bed. She removed her clothes quickly.

"I'm not sure we should."

"Why? Is it because you're Orthodox?"

It was because I wasn't over Aliza.

"Yes."

"You can't do girls?"

"I can't even touch them."

"Maybe you should go, then."

I did.

Jan. 20, 2007

I'm not sure how I got here. You walk in and there are a bunch of Purell dispensers and fabric seats, and you walk up to the glass partition, and the women behind it are busy making copies. Finally, one glances up at you – as if *you've* done something wrong – and says, "Hold on a second." And you nod, and say, "Sure," as if it were really no problem. But of course it's a problem. You're fucking visiting Student Health. Who goes there without a problem? So you wait. Finally, the woman in the butterfly scrubs – because they love rubbing these happy-go-lucky designs in your face – sits her largish bottom on the Staples chair with the pneumatic lever, looks up from the computer screen and says – doesn't ask, *says* – "What's your name?"

"Jeremiah," you say. "Jeremiah Goldstein."

"Could you spell that for me?"

"J. E. R. E—"

"Could you start again?"

I don't know how I got here. They got me sitting in the waiting area in the back now – the one for people who technically are no longer waiting but of course are still waiting because the doctor's busy. That's the racket. They bring you back and have a nursing student take your temperature and blood pressure. Then just when you think you'll see a doctor, you're brought to this cramped corner with no magazines and a couple of pamphlets about AIDS. There was a guy here a few moments ago who was coughing so violently they masked him. Now it's just me and a girl on her cell phone. "I'm gonna try to go out tonight anyway," she keeps saying.

How busy could Dr. Rogers be? Are there really that many other students with erectile dysfunction? I guess he treats other ailments. He is the sports medicine guy. Still. The pills aren't working. I popped one just before I hopped in bed with Lily the other night. The whole thing makes no sense, though. It's not like in the commercials where the pill allows you to be ready. The pill needs like 30 minutes to take effect. So I slid my arms under Lily on the couch, scooped her up and deposited her on the bed. Then, when she was ensconcing herself in the duvet, I poked my head into the closet and grabbed the orange bottle from my dopp kit. Then I had to try and distract her for 30 minutes. I kept asking her about weird things – like her favorite radio shows and silent cinema stars. Finally, she turned me over and damn near jumped me. I had to ask her about things she actually cares about – which was terrible, because now she thinks I like her. I never wanted to know about her favorite hometown burrito stand. Eventually, I turned over to the clock and saw 30 minutes had elapsed.

Then I still had to use my hand just to prop it up.

It's not funny. Sure, I try to be funny when I write about it, and I used to make all the stupid jokes. Bob Dole – *haha* – hardened criminals who steal it and face stiff penalties – *haha*. But when you can't get it up, you're lying in bed and the girl just looks at you strange, as if there's something terribly, terribly wrong. And maybe there is, you think, which is almost worse than the look itself. And if she doesn't look at you, if she figures out what's going on but refuses to say something out of care and politeness, you just feel that much worse. Because you know inside she knows, and she's not saying something partly out of pity – and the handicapped hate to be pitied. And she's going to go home to her friend Jen later and tell her and they're going to giggle no matter how nice they are. And they'll pity you.

It really has nothing to do with symbolism. It doesn't bother me that I am the figure of impotence – that I am the man who cannot construct and create. Poets care about symbolism. I just want to be able to do it, want to be able to feel free and reckless and wild. That's the fear that comes along with embarrassment: that you'll never experience spontaneous pleasure again. That what's fun for others will be a chore for you. That you'll never have an outlet for all that bothers you, and you'll have to slowly burn alone, never able to release everything the way everybody else can. I'm 19 – so that's the fear. It's not kids – although I do want kids, of my own, no offense to those who adopt, but I want to look in my boy's eye and see me – that precocious twinkle that comes from deep within. The thing we pass along. I do want that. But more than anything now, I just want to be able to be naughty.

Where is Dr. Rogers?

Maybe it's the naughtiness thing. Rogers thinks it could be in my head, since there's nothing functionally wrong with me, as far as he can tell. Maybe I just don't respond to promiscuity. Maybe I need a more serious connection. I told Rogers I wasn't over Aliza. I did tell him. Maybe he is right – maybe I *should* go to Psychological Services. That would be the ultimate capitulation, in a way. The ultimate admission. I've already come here to say I can't get it up. I'll go there and say I can't get my head straight and the circle will be complete. I will have conceded to dysfunction of the most important human systems. I will have conceded to being a total and utter wreck.

That's what Mo would say if he knew about all this. He already thinks I'm a wreck and he has no clue about the ED because I haven't told him. But he already thinks I'm messed up, going around on Friday nights drinking myself silly and punching walls and passing out on the floor of his apartment. He knows I stay up weeknights drinking bad coffee and eating fish sticks and watching Hitchcock movies broadcast on the college film station. And then I wake up the next day tired out of my mind and I have a pounding headache and all I can do is stay on the couch and pour another cup of coffee and watch "Garden State" and cry. Maybe I should tell Dr. Rogers about my sleeping habits. Maybe that can affect erections. I really hope so. It would make me feel better.

I trust Dr. Rogers even though I just met him a couple weeks ago. He's short – like 5'6" – and he has stringy blonde hair, metallic glasses and a nasal intonation. I'm not sure what it is about that combination, but I don't think I could feel more any more comfortable revealing my penis than I already do. It's funny. With this sort of problem you want to tell no one and everyone at once. In a way, I kinda desire pity – or no, not pity, but the sort of intrigue that such sexual problems tend to arouse. When they first bring me into the nurse's room, and this little student who's only a year older than I am – and very attractive – squeezes the pump in her delicate hand and the wrap tightens around me like a snake, I just want to say, "Hey, you know I'm here for erectile dysfunction, right?" I want to see her reaction. What she would say.

The thing about Student Health is the way it forces you to confront your lifestyle. Every time I come in they ask me whether I smoke, and the answer is no. But they also ask how often I drink and how sexually active I am. And the answer to the first question increases with each visit and the answer to the second is relatively inconstant, and I'm forced to say, if only to myself, "So long as someone's willing to come back to my room, I'll be active." Those are depressing truths. It was the suddenness of the end, I think.

Aliza and I spent the entire summer together, and part of the year before that. Then, boom, she arrives back on campus and she wants me to stab myself. Is that normal? Gosh, how I want to tell Mo about that in a story. That would feel good — telling him. I need that.

I continue scribbling on the small notebook I carry with me in the pocket of my corduroy pants. The girl across from me just ended her call. This place has a certain smell, I think.

"Goldstein," a brusque woman calls out from down the hall. "Goldstein."

I enter the office as if it's my house. Might as *well* act like this, I think. I *am* being seen for erectile dysfunction. I drape my olive winter jacket on the chair and place my sweatshirt over it and the scarf on top. I'm in a t-shirt now, and it's much airier. I grab the side of the little bed with the paper sheet and vault myself on. My long legs dangle and my toes scrape the floor. I exhale, and my stomach sinks and my back hunches over. I feel a stinging dryness in the bottom of my eyes, which are bluish from lack of sleep. If I squint, my contact lenses will pop out.

"Hi, again," Dr. Rogers says, sliding in the opening between the door and the frame. I hadn't closed it, for fear of what students in the hall might think if they saw someone shutting a door for privacy.

"Yes," I say. "Always good to see you."

The doctor half-smiles. I can't tell whether that's his subtle appreciation, or whether it's his not so subtle discomfort. They're inscrutable, these doctors. Always veiling themselves.

"So what's news?"

ny's voice say. I took another step,
s passenger door. The window was
ok.
-job.
nd blue tattersall shirt and a washed
lown, his hairless legs a creamy yellow
sitting spread-eagle, his knees pressed
l, his dick at the vertex. It didn't stick
lly — but curled back, onto his belly,
o much as a big coat hook, or the left
e in Picasso's "The Dream." His brown
n under his hat, a rat-tail like Kostya
back, and he was grinning like an idiot,
ine nose like a knife's edge.
ng on the bench next to him, bent over
red to the floor, like a defensive lineman
ack of her hair was flaxen and shimmery.
r blouse and a pleated miniskirt.
en.
guy urged, not noticing me.
mouth, like a bird sipping from a fountain.
he white swirl of her scalp.
l.
nd down, as though searching for apples in
hand on one of her thighs, gripping it as a
aint does bodies, or the cuff of a
r does arms.
e asked — and I wondered how he thought
what with her mouth being filled with him.
anaged.

"Actually, nothing."

"You've been taking the pills."

"Yes."

"You've been drinking a lot?"

"Not— yes. But not when I use the pills."

"You're not supposed to drink grapefruit juice with them, you know."

"I remember."

"And you're not getting it up? Or it's not staying up?"

"Both."

"Oh."

"At this point, there's not really much else I can do. Again, as we discussed, it might be useful for you to visit Psych."

"I've been thinking about it."

"And in the meantime, you can double the dosage, if you want, and take two pills."

"What about the other drugs — would they be more effective? What about the one you take in the morning that lasts all day?"

"You don't want that."

"Why?"

"I know it's cold now and everyone's buttoned-up. But how would you like it when the spring comes and the girls walk around in tank-tops and mini-skirts and everyone you see on the Alley gives you an erection?"

I imagine it. It seems wonderful. There I am, striding proudly down the main campus thoroughfare. I catch sight of a short blonde girl with tanned, thick thighs. I look over my left shoulder, fixating on her pleated, tartan mini. She notices my stare and I nod, as if to confirm my bold lustiness.

She grins.

"You're right," I mutter, only partially suppressing the resentment. "I wouldn't want that."

about
writhi
I shud
having
stale ex

But
It wa
dryer, an
wires fron
system to
since we v
lead to a g
night. I jerl
sliding door
two steps. Su
on the right
Plymouth.

"Yeah, bal

I stepped a
three or four l
empty beer bot
party. Trying to

The ceiling's
windshield, creati
been burnt there.

"Mmm," I heard a g
inching closer to the car
lowered. I bent down to l
He was getting a blow
A guy in a yellow-a
baseball cap – his pants
like buttered bread – was
up against the dashboar
out, the dick – not rea
resembling not a dick s
side of the woman's fac
bangs poked out from
Tszyu's stuck out the
his eyes glassy, his aqui
The girl was kneeli
his cock, her head squ
before the snap. The l
She had on a seersuck
Her face was hidd
"Keep going," the
She lowered her
He looked down at tl
"My, my," he sai
She bobbed up a
a vat. He had his lef
roller-coaster restr
sphygmomanomete
"Is that fun?" l
she might respond.
"Mom," she m

GABRIEL OPPENHEIM 110

GABRIEL OPPENHEI

And then, suddenly, she rose from his lap, pulling away her mouth, which was strewn with yarns of saliva. I could finally see her face. She was gazing straight at me. I was horrified. Her eyes were not eyes. Pearls or marbles, maybe, but nothing that could admit light. Her pupils were so small as to be nearly dots. Her irises blots of ink. Her face was not a face – it was a distant-looking thing, bluish like bad cheese, with a kind of sour edge, an almost twisted, puckered appearance, as though it were being pulled back, like a ponytail, or a wet rag squeezed dry.

She looked like a zombie – a glazed, half-dead wanderer.

"Hey, you wanna fuck?" the guy asked in a Southern twang.

The girl turned to him with bright, camera-flash eyes.

"Oh, yes," she said, clearly, and without a slur.

Without noticing me, they began to remove what was left of their clothing. The guy kicked his heels one against the other, like someone knocking muck from his boots before entering the house on a winter day, to slide his pants from his ankles. The girl undid the buttons on her blouse with such care – pushing them through the holes with the tips of her nails – that what small doubts I still had about her comprehension were removed. As she raised her shoulders forward – letting the blouse slide off her arms like a preening Nike of Samothrace – I caught sight of a tattoo between her shoulder blades, just beneath the clasp of her bra. It was a heart bisected by a cross, under the letters "WWJD."

The most excruciating part was the descent of her panties down her thighs. They were lacy and teal, composed of intricate netting that seemed to go on in its spiraling, spider-like pattern forever, like an arabesque on the side of a Moorish temple, with a little bowtie on the waistline. Their removal seemed irrevocable, and I watched them fall to the floor like a hovering leaf, watched them come to rest with finality on the rubber floor mat, next to the guy's white cotton beater and his beat-up Sperry Top-Siders.

The guy laid himself down over the entire bench (for the front seats were connected, not separated by a shifter), propping his penis up like some trashy American version of the Eiffel Tower. The girl lowered herself onto him like a hesitant child dipping a toe into a cold pool. I could hear the small air bubbles, formed inside his pre-cum, pop as she slithered down his member and settled her thighs around his love-handles.

A mad look flashed across his face. He reached his hands up, as Frankenstein's monster climbing off the doctor's table, and groped her breasts, which hung over him like the round discs you sometimes see in the mouths of African tribal women. She gave off a slight neighing sound, like a horny Mr. Ed.

Then they began to fuck – hard, rough and without mercy. He held her buttocks and slammed her down onto his cock and she shouted and moaned and jabbed at her clit with two fingers pushed together.

"Ohhhhhhhh," she screamed, but it was uneven – as though she were sitting over the axle of a particularly tightly-sprung school bus, her whole body vibrating with each passing pothole.

"You like that?" he asked. "You like that?"

Her head was already bobbing up and down, and he took its continued motion as confirmation that, yes, she did. They fucked like animals. At one point he started slapping her thighs, as though he had found something she said funny. The neighing had become a deep, spasmodic braying – had become an almost asthmatic reflex, a deep guffawing, a full-chested bellow, coarse and husky like hyperventilation, or a radiator stuffed with cotton. It sounded as though she were gasping for her life, as though his cock were painful and piercing, slicing through her bodily interstices – her organs and arteries and tissues.

"Oh, fuck! FUCK!" she shrieked, and she grabbed the two sides of her hair like a horse's reins and pulled them furiously – as though the horse were plowing ahead into a brick wall, and she doing her all to stop it. She was tugging so hard it seemed she'd rip the follicles from their sockets, uproot the entire scalp, like a gardener uplifting sod. Her eyes narrowed into a squint, and her face seemed to scrunch – as though she were about to cry. The lines of intensity, like taut ropes, appeared all over her face: on the side of her eyes, around the corners of her lips, on her ridged brow. Her whole body was tensed, like that of a man who, afraid of needles, is about to be injected. She was squeezing herself – bracing each second for the further projection of his sharp cock into her insides. The veins bulged from her neck, the striations of her traps– the seeming strands of her very muscle fibers – burst from her skin. She appeared she might pop out of her flesh.

"FUCK! FUCK!" she screeched.

Her hard nipples pointing outward like antennae, she grabbed at her breasts with insane vigor. She cupped them, yanked them, pinched them, rubbed them. She gathered them in her hands like soft fruit and pushed them together, dipping her chin, as though to submerge her whole face in the cleavage.

"FUCK! FUUUUUUUCK!"

She got louder, wilder. She was bouncing off him now each time he thrust – her body swaying this way and that, as a riding cowboy's. Her head knocked against the car's headliner but she didn't pause. The guy was making a snarling sound through his nose, almost like a bull. Underneath her high-pitched squeals, he was huffing, and puffing, breathing gusty-hot exhalations, like small, dusty Santa Anas.

"Aww," he moaned, pumping into her, and she keeled forward onto his chest, breaking her fall with an outstretched hand, which slapped his chest with a voluble smack and left a bright red mark below his pecs.

"Yes-fuck!" he screamed, and so he thrust again, and again she slapped him across the chest. It continued: Fuck-pump slap. The rhythm was in that stage when it becomes its own entity – when the very motion, apart from any purpose, becomes itself the thing –the means, elevated by mutual repetition, into a tantric ritual.

Fuck-pump-slap.

It was all they knew at that moment, all they could ever want to know.

She began to scream and curse.

"AWW, YOU SONOFABITCH!"

She grabbed his sunburned bicep to steady herself. "Aww, BITCH, BITCH."

I thought of Aliza. I had never done anything like this with her. How I wish I could now. Because it would be with her. And somewhat violent. And so far from the *shomeret* behavior she had once observed.

They paused. He took a deep breath. Her chest rose and fell, struggling to catch up to her heart. My nose twitched, and I smelled nearby banana peels.

After a couple moments' rest, he peeled her off him and spread her on all fours. Pulling her legs aside – as a surgical retractor – he inserted himself from behind and pumped her.

"Oh, yeah. Fuck me that way."

So he did, rocking her back and forth, his balls slapping the underside of her belly. They swung like the pendulum of a grandfather clock. I couldn't believe he hadn't cummed yet.

The girl stretched her arm out to rub her clit.

"Ohhhh," she groaned. "Ohhh."

"Yes, fuck me."

My dick tingled and rose inside my pants. I thought of Aliza.

He was getting closer now. His cheeks were flushed and he jerked forward, as though trying to push out the cum.

"Ahhhh!"

He rammed her so hard from behind that she collapsed forward, her arms beneath her, her head collided with the sideboard. It recoiled with a dull thud and spittle fell from her lips. Her head came to rest on the seat's transverse seam. Her eyes shut and she didn't move. A river of saliva began to course from her gaping mouth.

He didn't notice.

"Ahhh!"

He thrust into her, again and again. She was limp. He squeezed her love handles, for grip. He banged her one last time, hard, and cummed. Slowly he withdrew his dangling, glazed dick. He exhaled onto her back. He dismounted and began roaming the foot well for his pants. His body out of the way, I saw over her still-limp, still-lifeless body, through my window and then out the window on the other side, a video camera. One of those early-'90s, bulky black pieces, with the flashing red light on top and the mini-cassette deck on the side. A long, spindly hand was gripping it, the index finger on the record button.

"Did you get it?" asked the guy without pants.

"Yup."

"All of it – even the end?"

"Even the end."

"You motherfuckers!" I shouted.

They turned to me, nonchalantly.

"Oh. Hi."

"Oh? Hi? What's wrong with you?"

I ran out, back into the party whose excesses had led me to the garage, for fresh air.

Feb. 1, 2007

Vern and I raced down the staircase and into the night. We were running from the high rise. We both had forgotten about Shani's hearing. I had agreed to speak on her behalf – as both a member of another student group with funding – the newspaper – and a fan of her work. We looked both ways before entering the Alley, not for safety purposes but because we had no idea where the hearing was.

"Seamus Hall," I said. "It's in Seamus Heaney Hall!"

"You moron! That's not a lecture hall. It's a poet!"

"Well, I'm lost. I don't know what to do."

"Just follow me."

So I did, chasing after his wiggling legs, which had a funny if effective way of propelling him forward, like those feet on the wind-up toys McDonald's includes in its Infarcto-meals. I was terribly drunk. Aliza's face kept appearing before my eyes, and as those balls were actually trained on Vern, I knew I was delusional.

"Jeremiah, hurry up!"

I tumbled through the night, under the claws of the black trees and the frozen clouds above them. My steps on the ground were like single drops of water, fallen from a ceiling. Each one sounded tinny.

"Jeremiah! Where are you? Hurry up!"

I ran ahead. My left shoe snagged between two stones and I fell. Recovering, I plowed forward at twice the speed. Buildings began to be reduced in my blurry vision – to rectangles and squares. Their colors – even the serpentine green – became long horizontal bands, as in Ellsworth Kelly's train painting.

"Get yourself together. We're here."

I looked up – it was Sherman Hall, a large gothic building with heavy columns at its base. We didn't enter through these but curled around to the other side, where we'd have access to the basement lecture hall in which all SAC meetings, Vern now recalled, took place.

He twisted the metal knob.

"And that's why I should be allowed to keep running my magazine," said Shani, who was standing before the crowd in a blue halter dress. It showed off her breasts. Her forehead was damp. She eyed Vern, then sighed.

"But don't take my word for it! My good friend, who will now argue the case, has finally" – here she eyed Vern again – "and with my charming boyfriend" – a final mean look – "arrived."

She took a seat in the first row and I took the podium.

"I'm Jeremiah Goldstein," I said. "You might know from me the school newspaper, although I doubt that. I'm here to say something about my friend Shani and her magazine." Here I paused – and thought of Aliza's knife.

"I'm...er....Jeremiah Goldstein," I began again. "I've already told you why I'm here." I looked up at the crowd and noticed a silver RAZR cell phone that looked suspiciously like a knife.

"I'm," I began again, "the former boyfriend of Aliza Zuckerman. Maybe you know her. She's in a sorority now, or so I'm told. Spends a lot of time with those friends. Apparently they make her happy." Here I began to choke back tears. "And well, you should keep Shani's magazine. Without it, people like me wouldn't know who their exes were dating. Wouldn't know anything about that guy Jeff with his stupid European shoes and greasy hair and" – I began to weep openly – "and I'm sorry, about this" – sniffle, sniffle   "I just can't help it. I miss her. I'm sorry. Shani" – and here I turned to her with my eyes wet and my face pale – "I'm sorry I can't help you. Your publication deserves a better defender."

I looked her at one last time – long enough to see a scowl and a tear from Vern by her side – and ran to the door of the hall, but not before the food rising within me – the detritus of Rosie's meal, particularly her meatballs – scalded my throat with its acid and burbled from my mouth in a mucous stream of Campbell's-like chunky vomit.

The gloop splattered the SAC members in the first row, on whose shirts the flotsam stuck, like sticky rice on seaweed, and left a long salmon-colored trail on the floor. Outside the hall I keeled over and vomited twice more. It smelled like bologna. My chest rose and fell rapidly, and I could hear a janitor scrub a nearby bathroom with a wet mop.

Everything went dark.

****

My eyes didn't seem to open so much as be opened, by the weak light of a nearby lamp, which curling into them, slippery and soft, was like the gentle touch of a new mother. The room was dark, covered in shadows. I looked up, into the half-lit face of the boy above me, whose hands I now felt warm on my own. He was leaning over me, curled as an Ocean Spray wave, and he seemed to me a kind of protective canopy against whatever forces had leveled me so very low. My head pounded and my throat tasted of bad tuna fish.

"Where am I?"

"Your room."

He brought a finger to his lips, as if to indicate I should be still, and so I was, as he bent over the covers and pulled them up to my dry chin, which felt as if it had been recently scrubbed. He nodded to me, and I tried lifting my head to do the same, but it was too heavy.

A deep silence came over the room, such as those that follow long exhalations and lapping waves. There was only the distant hum of the refrigerator in the kitchenette, and the whirring of the computer hard-disk in my laptop. The light of the desk lamp set a kind of aura behind the boy, who I now noticed was on my desk chair, which he had lowered to the level of the twin extra-long bed. His face was soft, almost round, and its shadows gave him the shaded look of a long-unshaven beggar. He was in a burgundy sweater and neatly pressed grey slacks. He looked into my eyes with a moist sort of empathy. Around him the room seemed alive with particles of floating dust.

"Why am I here?"

"You shouldn't be talking."

Pause.

"Apparently, you vomited at Shani's hearing. Then, when Vern went to grab you, you pulled a flask from his coat – which I didn't even know he had, by the way – and had two more shots. Then, on the way back to the high-rise, you vomited again. One time on the tampon statue."

"That's pretty good aim."

"Yeah, it is."

He slid the pillow out from under my head and fluffed it. Mo was a nice guy after all.

"You know, I was about to close the deal."

"With that girl?"

"Yeah. I had gotten her pretty wasted."

"You didn't stop for me?"

"I did. Vern burst in, dragging you. I had to do something."

"But the girl…"

"I told her I'd see her another time and busted."

"But not literally?"

"No. Not literally. But it's alright. There will be other opportunities."

"I hope so."

I looked down at my belly and noticed a stain on my shirt. It was so nice to have Mo above me – caring for me. We could talk now.

"I vomited on myself?"

"A lot."

"Beautiful."

"Yeah."

He look at me. We laughed.

"I carried you up here on my back. Which, incidentally, is also covered in puke." Here he twisted in his seat, so that I might obtain a look.

"I'm really sorry."

"I told you already. It's no big deal."

Perfect – if it wasn't a big deal we could commence the discussion. There was so much I hadn't told him – about Aliza's weird needs, about the terrible dates I had been on – and I felt I needed to tell him.

"Why did you and Aliza break up?" he asked. It was sudden. I was caught off-guard.

"I dunno…I was just…"

He nodded. It was so easy for him just to ask these things and be in the moment. I had fucked up. I couldn't tell him now. I didn't feel I could at least.

"Tell me a bedtime story," I said.

"Are you serious?"

"Don't be a tough guy."

"Once there was a boy named Mo. He went to school and had a good time. The end."

My eyes closed. He was still over me – I could feel his warm breath.

"You want a story?"

As my eyes were closed, and I was doing my best simulation of dream-breathing, he was clearly talking to himself.

"I'll tell you a story. There was this one time, many years ago, when I was in sixth grade. And there was this one girl. Her name was Hannah. Hannah Meyerson. You want me to describe her? She was...uh...about 4'6" and very petite. She wore plaid a lot. Anyway I had a crush. A big crush..."

I kept quiet.

"It's hard for me to remember what it felt like. It wasn't like the way I like girls now. It was so much more exciting. And plus I was so much more hormonal. One time, we were with the *shul* on some youth bowling trip on a Saturday night, and that was exciting enough because I never went out on Saturday nights – we were in sixth grade. I spent Saturday nights watching SNICK– 'All That' and 'Kenan and Kel' and 'Roundhouse.' And 'Ren and Stimpy.' I *hated* 'Are You Afraid of the Dark?' That show scared me...

"We're out on a Saturday night on this old school bus which goes up and down with every little bump. She was sitting in the last row of the bus and I was in the second-to-last and I kept turning behind me to talk to her. And she barely said anything. I think she described her pets. It didn't matter. We were in the back of a school bus and it was dark and it was a Saturday night. I was so excited talking to her that I actually cummed in my pants against the seat. It wasn't a lot of cum, mostly pre-cum, but still. No conversation excites me now…"

I turned to my side, my breathing continuous. He was opening up. I had waited for this for so long. I felt all warm and flush.

"Nothing happened that night at the bowling alley. Actually, she kind of ignored me while we were there, which was unbelievably disappointing. The bus ride home sucked.

"We wound up dating. Three-quarters of the way into sixth-grade, it was spring. She came up to me at recess and just talked. I felt cool for staying on the side, while the other guys played football. I even took off my *tzizis*[11] in the morning and shoved them in my locker so she wouldn't be put off by the loose strings.

"We talked about MTV. 'TRL' was really big, then. I wanted to be Carson Daly. Or at least watch him in Times Square. And she wanted to kiss him. We talked about the music. Britney Spears was big. That was the year 'Hit me, Baby, One More Time' came out. And Kid Rock with "Bawitdaba." And Limp Bizkit was big – that's when everyone started buying that stupid Yankees cap. 'I did it all for the nookie' – remember? – 'so you could take that cookie and stick it up your yeah' We talked about the Backstreet Boys. We loved 'Millennium.'

"I asked her out the weirdest way. Now I wouldn't even it call it that because we never did go out, but going out had a different meaning to sixth-graders. You didn't actually have to take her anywhere. So I called her one day. I was in my parent's bedroom, using the phone by my mom's side of the bed. And I

---

[11] A ritual garment fringed with strings whose daily wearing is mandated by the Torah in the "*Sh'ma*" section.

remember half-leaning over the bed, kind of the way I am doing to you now. I was so nervous I had one hand around the telephone cord – just completely clenched. She came on and said hi and I said, 'I was talking to your friend Nicole.' Because she had this friend Nicole. 'I spoke to Nicole and she said I should ask you out.' And then the phone went silent and that was it. I didn't say anything else. It was just dead. And she was obviously expecting me to continue. But I didn't say anything. She had to break the silence and say, 'Are you asking me out?' I said yes.

"She broke up with me on my birthday. In an email. It just goes to show how unjustified I was in my fears. There I was, thinking I was the only kid who didn't know how to act like a grown-up, scolding myself for not having the balls to go ahead and ask her out and finally, when it came time for us to be adults about something and express our feelings, she couldn't do it either.

"I don't remember what the email said. I saw it first thing when I woke up. I printed it out and shoved it into the bottom drawer of my nightstand, figuring it was too important not to save. Funnily enough that stand had an earlier break-up note – this one handwritten by her friends – which she had delivered to me and then rescinded weeks earlier after I had made a naughty comment about one of her friends' t-shirts.

"There was one amazing night I shared with Hannah. It was late and cold, in the winter. She asked me on the phone to come over. My parents were asleep. So I bundled myself in a parka and gloves and snow boots and walked with nothing on me. Not a wallet, not a phone. I passed the old ice-cream shop and the jeweler's, and the shoe store. Finally, I reached the residential area where she lived and I climbed up the street. It a big, sloping hill. I got to her place and tiptoed to the back and I looked in the window and saw her asleep on the couch. I banged on the window and she woke up and opened up. She looked so perfect and young in her nightie. I stood there and stared. 'Aren't you coming in?' she asked, but I couldn't respond. 'Fine, if you're not gonna come in, I'll come out.' She slipped on her dad's slippers and wrapped herself in the blanket on the couch and she walked out, past me, toward the front yard. Now, you gotta understand, this didn't make any sense because her backyard had this nice swing you could sit on and the front yard didn't have anything except for the steps. But I followed her, and watched her butt sway in the nightie and she kept going, past the steps, toward the end of the driveway, where she sat Indian-style and looked up to the sky. 'You sure you want to sit down there? The concrete's gonna be cold.' 'Yeah.' I nodded and sat down behind her. My hands trembled and I slid them around her waist. She fell back, into me. 'Look at the stars.' 'They're winking at us.' The wind hit us. I squeezed her. 'I love you, Mo.' 'I love you, too, Hannah.' We leaned into each other and then our lips were touching and then I felt a long warm thing slither into my mouth."

I felt his hand pat me on the shoulder and hearing footsteps, opened my eyes. His back was to me and he was halfway out of the room. A great yawning sound came from the door, a whoosh, and then a final thud.

****

My forehead throbbed. My jaw was stiff and my throat dry. The room was cool. The down comforter made a crinkling noise. The computer droned like a prop plane.

I stretched out my arms.

Knock-knock!

I didn't move.

Knock-knock!

"Argh!"

I tramped to the door. I grabbed the knob and gave it a hard yank.

"Vern!"

"Jeremiah!"

"What are you doing here?"

"Given how sick you were last night, I could ask you the same."

"Fair enough. Come in."

The light fell on us softly as we walked into the bedroom. It illuminated the scruffy edges of his chin and the rough herringbone of his new sport coat. His Cole Haan loafers were beaten up just enough to be marbled. I began to undress.

"Should I put on a *Shabbos* shirt?"

"Sure. But we're not going to shul."

The fabric was soft on my body. I moved to the mirror to look at myself. I was awfully haggard: my eyes had the purplish bags which usually appear on boxers; my nose seemed somehow bigger than usual.

"You look fine. Let's go."

"I need to brush my teeth."

"Now? After dressing?"

"You got any better ideas?"

"Fine."

I grabbed the brush from its on-the-wall holder.

"*Shit.*"

"What?"

"What happened with Shani? I totally forgot."

"They voted to take away her funding."

"They did?"

"Yeah."

"I'm sorry." Pause. "I'm *so* sorry."

"It's okay. She's not mad."

"I fucked it up."

"Yeah, you did. Also, you have Colgate on your collar."

The walk to wherever we were heading was brisk. Vern swung alongside me like a tote bag. The air kept slipping between my lips and gums. Vern, his eyebrows raised, stared at me.

"I'm fine, Vern. *Really*...You can stop staring."

"Just checking. Anyway, it doesn't matter. Where we'll going will cheer you up."

"I should be cheering you – and Shani – after what happened...Where are we going?"

"Just follow me."

We continued along the Alley, which was filled with students in sweatpants on their Saturday errands. The girls were carrying bags from the tented bazaar up ahead, whose wares consisted of bracelets and jams. The boys were jogging in packs, in technical sport fleeces and earmuffs. Above us the trees were spindly walking sticks – the canes of hobbled professors and Gandalf-imitators.

"We're here."

"Here? This building?"

"Yes."

I looked up. It was College Hall, the campus' very first building.

"Come – we'll take the side entrance."

Vern stepped onto a winding stone path that ran from the front steps, around a weeping willow, and into a small door blocked by a brick gate.

"How do we get past this?"

"Never fear."

Removing a long brass key from his pocket, he pushed up against the brick – at the point of a small hole – and twisted. It swung open, revealing a dark staircase (each flight about two stories high) and a swarm of gnats.

"Voila."

"Impressive."

He swatted the bugs and ascended the stairs. I followed. My knees were sore and my back ached. The stairwell's tall, opaque windows let in a milky light. The air was heavy with dust. The white walls, mottled with green patches, smelled of mildew.

"Can we slow down?"

"Don't be a pussy."

After three flights, I leant over the rail and huffed. Below me was a dark spiral.

"This is endless. How many flights left?"

"Only one and a half."

"A half? How do you get a half?"

"You'll see."

He began taking the steps in twos. I trailed behind, my hand running along the banister. Finally I reached the top, where he was leaning against a red door, tapping his watch. Above him was a huge bronze lamp – unlit – and a thick rope of twine.

"Bell tower – don't pull it," he said. "In here."

He inserted the same key into the lock and twisted. What was revealed was a long hallway."

"I've been here before – these are just classrooms."

"Mostly."

He walked ahead and I followed. The hall was empty and smelled of books. The only light came from the stained glass windows at either end. We both looked blue in their shadows.

He unlocked a non-descript door I had always taken for a janitor's closet. We stepped forward, onto a red carpet stained in spots by black gunk.

"Tobacco. You know how intellectuals love to smoke."

I nodded. We were on a landing no larger than our combined footprints. Its walls were a rich dark wood, which smelled like the cedar chips one puts in the closet. These continued up the narrow staircase abutting the landing, both sides of which were covered in photographs and framed programs.

"Well, I might as well begin the tour here. This is the Zelosophic Society. The first rule of the Zelosophic Society is that you do not talk about the Zelosophic Society. The second rule is that, if I find out you did talk, I'll tell Shani you purposely ruined her presentation and I'll let her eat you alive."

"Okay, okay – deal."

"Good. Now, as we walk up, take a look at the photos and programs on the wall. The former are all the famous people who have come and spoken here and the—"

"Woody Allen spoke here last semester?"

"Yes."

"But I never heard about that."

"Such is the point. Our events are closed. That's why famous people are willing to come."

I gazed up the wall. The frames seemed endless – one row was topped by another and then another. They've must've run 20-feet high. There were gold sconces between the frames.

"This place is insane."

"I know."

We reached the top of the stairs. This floor was also carpeted in red, sided with mahogany and lit by golden lamps.

"All the society's rooms branch off this hall. There aren't many and they're all pretty much the same. Here – we'll start back there."

He walked to the left. I stepped in hesitantly. The room was so dim I could make nothing out.

"Is this the weaponry room?"

"Actually" – he flipped on the light switch – "this is our kitchen."

It was. There was a lot of Formica.

"We do all our own cooking for events."

"Oh."

"The people here are good at making salmon croquettes. Anyway, I'm messing with you. There's no reason to see this room. We'll move on."

We walked out into the hall and then into a gigantic circular reading room. The wall was covered in a bookcase. All the books were bound in red.

"Yeah," Vern said, catching my look, "we re-bind all our books."

I nodded and looked at all the spines: histories of the world, great American novels, essays on Italian film. At the far end of the case sat a huge wooden desk. Its legs were the legs of a lion and the top was shiny. It supported yet another desk – this one much smaller – which was slanted and made of bamboo. On top of that was just one book, open to a page about a quarter of the way in and illuminated by an old-fashioned clerk's lamp of gold and green-glass.

Vern walked to it.

"Come," he said.

We stood over the book.

"I want you to read this."

"What is it?"

"It's an old Japanese novel. From the 17th-century."

"Okay."

I bent over and squinted.

"I can't make this out. It's too dark."

I brought my nose against the bumps of the ink.

"'Live for the moment, look at the moon, the cherry-blossom and maple leaves, love wine, women and poetry, encounter with humor the poverty that stares you in the face and don't be discouraged by it, let yourself be carried along on the river of life like a calabash that drifts downstream, that is what *ukiyo* means.'"

I asked him what ukiyo was. He said it was Japanese for "floating world."

"Floating world?"

"Yeah."

He walked behind me and then said, "I got another one — hold on."

He left the room. I could hear his footsteps at first, then not all. Every motion in this building seemed muffled. I tapped my finger on the bamboo. He returned.

"Here."

He dropped a huge book onto the open one before us. Dust flew into the air.

"This one's a British translation of hieroglyphics."

"How do you find these things?"

We laughed. He threw open the cover. He was clearly searching for a specific page so I asked him how he knew where to look in such a big book. He said he came here a lot. And then it hit me.

"Is this where you go during parties? Up *here* – to *read*?"

"Not even Shani knows," he said, "so don't say a word."

I promised not to and he pointed to a line.

I read: "'Canoeing in the papyrus beds, the pools of wildfowl, the marshes and the streams, spearing with the two-pronged spear, he transfixes thirty fish; how delightful is the day of hunting the hippopotamus.'"

Vern didn't say anything. He looked at me, expectantly. I told him I thought it was poetic. He said, "No, it's more than poetic. I've decided that the world can be reduced to two things – two ways of life. These two."

I said how.

He said, "The Japanese novel is what we should be doing. 'Live for the moment, look at the moon'…etcetera. And the Egyptian description – hunting the hippo – is how we actually live."

"Hunting the hippopotamus? That's what we do?"

"Yes. We hunt the hippopotamus."

To me, there was no difference between the passages and I told him so. "They both involve being in the moment and doing something," I said.

"One's a hunt and one's not," he said. "Think about it. One involves need."

March. 12, 2007

I was ready to tell Mo about how the breakup had gone down. I called him and said we needed to talk. He said, yeah, whatever, sure, we talk all the time. I said, no, it's about something specific. He said, what's the difference, specific, shmecific – we see each other all the time, we can talk the next time we see each other at lunch or something.

He didn't get it. He saw no urgency. Had no need to tell me anything. Truth is, as much as I wanted to tell him about the Aliza situation, I wanted to find out about him. What the hell was he up to now that he was single? Was he fucking miserable like me? Unlikely. Was he on Viagra, also? Even more unlikely.

I confronted him about it – I mean, the difference in our mindsets one day late at night. We were at Dave's, the sports bar. I was drinking this great mix from Yuengling – Half and Half, they call it.

"I gotta tell you what happened with Aliza," I said. And he was so nonchalant about it – he said, "Sure, bro, go for it" – that I felt no, I can't do this – especially not here, in a bar.

I needed him to make a commotion about it – a real to-do – like, "Oh, yeah, I've been waiting for months to hear about this." And when I didn't get one I kind of doubted we were close at all.

March 15, 2007

The snow came down as though it knew we were cold and wanted to help. It carpeted every mound and bump in the landscape and then descended in another layer and then another, so that by the end, every piece of earth was bundled beneath several strata of densely pressed flakes, like a child cosseted with one blanket after another, in a house without heating, by a mother wary of the temperature of his skin.

All the hard edges were smoothed.

I had sent a text message. I was sitting on the radiator by the window, looking at the snow. My phone screen was blank. I fidgeted. Getting up, I stretched, then moved to the refrigerator. Inside was only orange juice and an empty salsa jar.

"I love you."

It was back on my screen. I had involuntarily clicked over to Sent Messages. The fridge door was ajar. I slammed it shut and jammed the phone into my sweatpants pocket.

I walked back to the sill. Well, I had sent it. It was done now. There was nothing I could do. It would be up to Aliza to respond.

A buzz.

I jabbed my hand into my pants.

"We should discuss this."

The blood rushed to my face. I felt dizzy. Was this a good sign? She at least wanted to discuss.

"Do you want to meet at Starbucks?"

"I can't. On Long Island for cousin's bat-mitzvah."

"Long Island???"

"Yes."

I thought for a moment. Mo had walked to Hannah's house in the cold. I could definitely drive it.

"I'm gonna come now."

"FROM SCHOOL?!"

"Yes. By car. The weather's not so bad."

"Jeremiah. *Don't.* It's not worth it."

What was she thinking? That I was going to spin out in the snow and die? And anyway, I thought that was what she wanted   she wanted me to hurt myself in some way – to commit an act of violence.

"No biggie. I enjoy driving in bad weather."

"Jeremiah. *Please.*"

"I'm coming."

Minutes passed without a response. Finally:

"Fine. But you must update me every 30 minutes, and, as you know, there's no place for you to stay."

****

The snow kept hitting my windshield in clumps. No longer was it falling from the sky but from the backs of big-rigs and SUVs. I gripped the wheel tightly and kept the radio on. If I died, it'd be to the classical music of WQXR. That seemed kind of funny.

The landscape before me was repetitive. The sky was a blue streak.

****

"I love you, Aliza, and I'll always love you, and there's nothing you or I can ever do about it."

She looked at me from the passenger seat. Her expression was so blank that I could hardly believe she was the passionate girl who has asked me to hurt myself or steal a laptop.

"Incidentally, is there anyway we can go inside the house? It's really cold."

She shook her head. Her long brownish hair brushed gently against her neck. Gosh, it was cold.

"Fine. I have nothing more to say. I love you, and that's the bottom line."

She frowned and stared into her lap. She was in a loose grey cotton top and black leggings. Her mouth opened, then closed again. She sighed. I turned from her, and looked out the driver-side window. A cat was licking itself in the street, just next to her cousin's mailbox. Suddenly I felt something warm on my neck. I turned. She was caressing my shoulders – waving her hands along my lats, up my neck and to my ears.

"Stop."

"I feel bad."

I pushed her hands away.

"I don't want you to feel bad. I want you to like me. And I want to get back together. And I don't want to steal."

She turned away, toward her own window. Her breath fogged it up.

"You know what I'm like. I have issues. You have to accept them."

"Will you work with me at least? And try to help yourself?"

She lowered her head, like she didn't want to see me. She didn't say anything. It was definitely a bad sign. I was hoping she'd agree at the very least to come to grips with this whole thing. Because that to me was the problem. There was no way she had stopped liking me.

"I'm not sure I still like you," she said.

I was shocked. I felt like I had been punched in the stomach. And then a sound came from the front door:

"Aliza?"

It was a man standing there, calling her. She left the car and as she did he came up to her.

"What are you doing out here in the cold?" he asked, gruffly. "And who is this?"

She stared at the ground.

"Sorry, Dad. I was just talking to a friend."

Dad? Friend? What the fuck? Her dad was alive? She had lied about that, too? This was all too much. And if this was her dad, was this also her home? Had she grown up here – only 30 minutes from where I had? Could that be?

"Aliza?" I called out to her. She didn't respond but walked inside.

I was left in the car, with the heat blowing over me. This was all too much.

She was so pathologically fucked. And I loved her so much.

April 17, 2007

My editor at the newspaper asked me what I wanted to write for my last column as a sophomore (I was leaving the paper in the hope that I'd get the Hutchinson mentorship and have to devote time to that; of course, I first had to get the thing and so it really mattered which topic I chose for my last column because it had to be damn good to impress him – it would be the last he looked at). I said I knew exactly.

I wrote a piece on what a roommate should or shouldn't do for the other guy in the apartment. I said the most important thing was sharing stories – because it seemed true. And I wrote about how the best moment I had had at school was the night I shared first masturbation stories with my roomie as a freshman and we had rapped the wall to communicate in a kind of unspoken way.

To me that was college.

April 18, 2007

"You sonofabitch!"

I looked up the staircase, my cup of coffee shaky in my hand. He was standing on the landing between the first and second floors. I really hadn't expected this.

"Look, Mo. Don't yell. Not here."

"Not here! This is the Jewish Center – it's the perfect place to yell."

He rushed down the stairs. We were face-to-face.

"If you want to talk about this, we should do it some place private."

"No, We're gonna talk here and now because this is exactly why I'm so upset. Everyone here now knows about me."

"They don't know anything."

He stepped away, almost as if there were a third person present with whom he was also talking.

"The thing I don't get it is how you could do it. I mean to write about your own best friend. And to throw in all the personal stuff. I didn't even tell you a masturbation story."

"I guess not."

That was a factual error. He was right. His story had to do with a girl named Tali.

"That's not even the point. The point is, you didn't ask permission to do it. You just did. And I don't get that."

"I was just writing the truth," I said. "We all need that sharing."

"*You* do," he said. "But don't speak for me. I'm at peace with things without making them all explicit. And now" – he looked around – "I'm not gonna be able to walk around campus without people thinking I'm some weird soul-bearing loser."

April 20, 2007

I knocked gently on his door, afraid that the slightest disturbance would rouse him from a serious literary reverie. A creak came from within — maybe the sound of a chair falling back on an ungreased axle.

"Hello?"

No answer.

"Um, Mr. Hutchinson, sir?"

"Jeremiah?" came a gentle voice.

I opened the door a crack.

"Yes, it's me. I've come for our meeting."

There was the sound of footsteps and then the crack was filled with a robust man in a sweater and khakis and a pair of Doc Marten's. He was pale, with a thin white beard and two tufts of hair on his head like cotton balls.

He smiled.

"It's good to finally meet you. Formally, I mean."

"Thank you."

He smiled again and waved his hand toward the room behind him. We walked in. The room wasn't big, but it was decorated in a cozy way: On the floor was a rug. The wall to my left was lined with a long sofa and several art prints. The other wall was one continuous bookshelf, reaching from floor to ceiling, with a horizontal pole and a ladder.

"Pull up some sofa. Make yourself at home."

I looked down at the cushions on which I was about to fall and kind of just let go. I fell back onto them with a poof.

"I'll be very brief because you're probably nervous. You got it."

I jumped off the couch and reached to shake his hand.

"Thank you!"

He laughed.

"Okay, that's enough. We've got business to discuss."

I sat back down.

"First, I just want to say something about the competition. It was tough this year. And to be perfectly honest, I wasn't even sure a couple months ago that I was gonna do the fellowship at all. I've been pretty busy lately with my own work and I wasn't certain I had it in me. It takes a lot of work. You have to talk to the kids constantly."

He smiled.

"But you convinced me. I liked your stuff freshman year. It struck me as very sincere – in a good way. A couple months ago I felt you were losing your way a little bit. Maybe I was just reading into things, but your columns started to sound defensive, as if you felt the need to prove yourself.

"But that's in the past now. Let's discuss our big project. You have any ideas as to what you might wanna do?"

He looked up. I swallowed.

"Not really…"

"That's normal. We'll think about it in the next few days and…"

"Actually, no – I *do* have an idea."

"Oh?"

"It's a floating world kinda thing."

"Floating world?"

"It's a Japanese concept. About the fleetingness of life. I wanna do something like that. Something sort of brief."

"Okay, we can work off that, I guess."

"Something maybe like '36 Views of the Quad.' A written equivalent of a series of prints."

"Hmm. What would the written equivalent be?"

"Vignettes? Maybe 36 little scenes?"
"Nice. Little interactions. I like it."
"I like it, too."

April. 21, 2007

"Why'd you do it, J?"

The rope made a whooshing sound. Vern watched me.

"I dunno."

It was a lie. I had made a choice. To be honest about my feelings.

"You must have some idea."

"Some."

The rope caught my left foot, and I landed on the right, as though doing the Lindy Hop. Vern grabbed it and began flicking his wrists. He was good.

"Where'd you learn to jump like that?"

"My school. We used to have a guy visit us. The rope guy, he was called."

He crossed it and uncrossed it. My eyes followed its path.

"Your yeshiva brought in a jump-roper?"

"I didn't go to a yeshiva. It was a private school."

"Oh, I forgot."

The rope looped around his left leg and pulled his thigh.

"Okay, I'm done here."

"It's like this," I said, taking the rope. "I thought he'd like it."

"Bullshit."

"No—"

"Be honest."

"Okay, I didn't know how he'd react. But I felt it. I felt it strongly. And for the first time in awhile I felt like I had something to say. I wasn't just writing to impress people. I had a message."

He frowned.

"By the way," I said. "Did I tell you Aliza lied to me about her dad? He's alive."

Vern nodded. "Shani told me. Also, you should know about Mo – *his* dad is sick."

I had heard. Shani had told me.

Junior Year

Sept. 2, 2007

I drove down myself. No parents – just an open sunroof and wind in my hair. When I got there I parked and opened the trunk. As I leaned in I felt someone approach.

"Welcome back, J."

It was Vern.

"Hey, V. What's up?"

He looked behind him, over his right shoulder. His right hand combed through his neat black hair and he mumbled.

"We gotta go."

I knew then that Mo's dad had finally died.

****

I wrote another Quad vignette on the plane down to Atlanta.

"She steps back, against the fireplace, and looks out the window, onto the grassy courtyard below. All of the Quad's little dramas are now spilling over, into this shared area: there's another couple bickering in the northernmost corner, and he looks about to cry; nearer, by the statue of the first provost, on the shaded bench, are two boys muttering and cursing.

"Anita turned from the window, back toward Shane. 'No, I can't forgive you,' she said, her head bowed forward. He stepped ahead and lifted her chin in his hand. 'Here. Take this.'

Her eyes had closed but now they were open and she saw the knife in his hand.

"Plunge it into me," he said. "I want you to wound me."

****

The funeral home was actually across the street from the Petco, only we hadn't been able to spot it from our side of the road. It was a long white chapel with a roof that slanted on either side and met in a point in the middle. The outside walls were completely white. Vern kept raising his eyes toward it, only to lower them back to the ground.

"Are we gonna go in?" I asked.

He nodded, took a step forward, then paused.

"I can't...yet."

I looked at my watch.

"We'll give it a couple more minutes."

Click.

Vern and I looked to our left. There was a half-empty parking lot and a long black Town Car limo that had just pulled in. A large brunette woman, dressed in black, was climbing out the back. Her face was creased and red and puffy. We watched her. She pushed off the grey leather seat and stood, but the sun seemed to blind her and she squinted, before taking a few steps forward. Then she shook her head and staggered back to the car. She folded over, her arms splayed on the car's roof, and began to sob. The tears rolled down her cheeks, onto her arms and off her body, onto the sticky gravel.

Meanwhile another person was exiting the limo. Also a woman, much older-looking, maybe in her 80s. She had long white hair that mirrored the contours of her ragged black dress. Her face was like the bark of a tree near a high school – one that has been carved and engraved by young couples. She stepped out and looked to her left, toward the woman crying on the roof. She sighed, and, her head raised, stepped over and patted the woman on the back of the head. Her lips moved, and it looked like she also whispered something.

Next came a small boy – probably 10 or 11 years old. His hair was cut short to his head and he had big ears and large, brown eyes, but his lips were pursed and his cheeks seemed swollen and heavy. He peeked out, looking to his right, at the women curled up over the car, and to his left, at Vern and me standing silently on the corner, and then fell forward – not even extending his legs but just tumbling out of car as if doing a cannonball.

"Jacob!"

The heavy woman pushed the older woman off of her and rushed to the ground. The boy was still balled up, his hands gripping his tucked-in legs. She brushed his little hair off his forehead and felt his skin.

"Are you bleeding? Are you okay?"

The boy looked at her and didn't say anything. His eyes were vacant.

"Answer me, Jacob! Are you okay?"

The boy shook his head and scowled.

"I'm not telling you."

"You have to tell me, Jacob. I need to know whether you're okay."

"No. I'm not saying anything to you – only to daddy. Bring him back."

The woman looked down at the boy and then away, and the tears began falling from her face again, and she rushed back to the side of the car and grabbed at the older woman, for balance.

Her knees buckled, and the old woman's bony arms propped her up.

Meanwhile another head appeared in the dark opening of the car door. It was a young man's face – with ringed eyes and tousled dirty-blonde hair. The head pushed its way forward and then the neck was visible – long and veiny – and a rumpled black suit that hung from the body like a shawl. As the body rose into the air one long leg emerged from the car and then another.

And then the young man was standing, looking over the scene – the two women curled up over one another on the car, the boy balled-up on the ground, all of them now shrieking – with a stern, cold look, his upper teeth sunk hard into his lower lip. He took a deep breath, let his arms fall to his side, and began to walk ahead, past the car, across the freshly-painted white lines of the parking lot, toward the steel door at the side of the building. Vern and I watched him cross all these lines, watched him cut through the spring-like moist air, and watched him pull strongly as he threw open the side door. Then we saw him stop.

He turned his head to the right, to the area just over his shoulder and looked at us.

Vern nodded at him and he nodded back.

I tried to give a sympathetic smile. He stared at me – hard – and shook his head. So much for reconciling with Mo at his dad's funeral.

He grabbed the door handle and stepped into the chapel.

******

"How about there?"

Vern was whispering, pointing to the third row from the back on the left side.

"Fine," I said.

We walked out of the doorway and past the plain wooden casket propped up on a stand next to the podium – it was a light pine wood, with no glazing or anything, and it looked like a bunch of slats you might buy at Home Depot.[12] The front of the room had three big glass windows toward the top and they let in a light, spring air that fell on our faces. We walked down the red-carpeted aisle, toward the chairs in the back. On either side of us were older men and women in shoes with Velcro and big glasses. There were also younger people – blonde women in their 30s with their arms folded across their waists and men in dark, pinstriped suits and wide, striped ties.

Vern went into the row first and moved all the way down, so he was against the wall. I sat next to him.

"Look."

He pointed across the aisle, to the women's side of the room, about four rows ahead. Sitting there were Rosie, Shani and Aliza. Shani had a big black leather bag open on her lap and was fishing through it. Both Rosie and Aliza were bent over, their hands covering their faces. Finally Shani looked up and pulled her hand from the bag. It was clutching a big wad of tissues. She pulled three from the pile with her nails and handed them to Rosie and then did the same for Aliza. All at once they brought the tissues to their noses and blew.

I turned to Vern and shook my head. He was still looking at the girls. His eyes were teary. Suddenly he squinted hard, as if seeing something he couldn't quite believe. I turned back the other way. A girl was sliding into the row where Rosie, Shani and Aliza were. She was tallish, but not exactly tall, with

---

[12] Jewish law forbids coffin ornamentation.

thing without his glasses. He could never see in the pool, yet he managed to avoid the buoys. That was Henry.

"He spoke many languages. In cabs he'd often strike up a conversation with the driver in the driver's language. The driver was always shocked.

"He was a stickler for table manners yet he always managed to stain his shirt with barbeque sauce. And he loved pancakes.

"He was a good father."

Huh-huh-huh-huh.

Her head fell forward and she sobbed. Vern reached out and squeezed my knee cap, while still looking forward. I did the same to him.

"I'm sorry…One second."

She bent over and hobbled to the front row. The old woman from the parking lot stood up. They embraced. Their sobs were muffled in the old woman's heavy cloth dress.

Huh-huh-huh-huh.

I looked over to the girl's side. Aliza's head was buried in Caroline's lap. Her chest rose and fell with each of her own sobs. A man in a shabby grey suit and black leather sneakers – the kind that poor rabbis wear instead of real dress shoes – rushed down the aisle.

He grabbed the microphone on the podium.

"We all have to understand the circumstances here." He looked down at the first row. The woman was now trying to tear herself away from the older women, reaching for the podium. "It's okay, Chanah," the rabbi said. "Your words were very beautiful and a tribute to your husband…We will now hear from Mo—"

"No – I'm not done!"

shimmering black hair and light-blue eyes. Her body, eve
dark black dress with sleeves to her elbows, was fa
slender, athletic and regal, with perfectly proportioned b
and the kind of ass you could hold in your hands. Her upt
nose hadn't changed, nor had the string of pearls alon;
milky-freckled neck.

Caroline.

"What the hell is she doing here?" I asked.

Vern shrugged.

"I dunno."

****

"I want to tell you something about my husband, ʒic
livracha.[13]" Mo's mom was speaking.

She brushed a dangling strand of hair off her forehead
sighed. Reaching into the pocket of her small black jacket
pulled out folded pages. She placed them on the woo
podium with one hand and ran the other along their width
then height.

"I am going to read."

She slid her hand back into her jacket and removed a sr
case. She flipped it open and took out a pair of glasses and v
calmly unfolded their stems and positioned them on her e
and nose. She put the case on the podium, above the pages, a
bent forward.

"These are just things. Facts.

"He was a swimmer in high school, back in the days bef
swimmers were tall and lanky. He was a barrel-chested m
There are funny pictures of him in those full-body swim trur
of the 1950s. He's usually smiling, but really, he can't se

---

[13] "May his memory be for a blessing."

She rushed to the podium and ripped the microphone from the rabbi's hand and placed it back in its silver arm. The pages were still there. She bent over and began in a quivering voice.

"He read many things, but mostly political magazines. He hated how vulgar language had become but he cursed frequently.

"Work was accounting. It was not a glamorous job and I think he wanted to do more. But things just sort of happened, and after the fact, he couldn't restart.

"His eyes had thoughts.

"His mother always said he'd be a Hollywood star. She's there – in the front row. Rose – I don't know what I'd do without you. You're the most supportive mother anyone could be and your son – my husband – he...his life was a testament to that...

"He was devout – not in showy ways, but quietly. He was recruited by one university to swim, but he didn't take it because the coach made an anti-Semitic joke during his visit. I think they thought he wasn't Jewish. He had a really straight nose.

"The only time I saw him cry was when Moshe – our first-born – was born."

******

The chazzan walked slowly. He passed the front row and looked back, at the family. He gave a sideways glance at the wooden box. He looked up, at the rows of people, then back down at the box. Still looking down he grabbed the microphone from its holder with his right arm.

He placed it on his lower lip and began to chant in a deep, doleful voice.

Kel molay rachamim, shochayn bamromim, ham-tzay m'nucho n'chonoh al kan-fey ha-shchinoh...[14]

****

"Will the pallbearers please come to the front of the room?"

I looked at Vern. He nodded. We stood. We shuffled out of the row, trying not to bang into people's knees.

I walked up the aisle. I felt people's eyes on me. Vern was by my side, to the right. I really didn't want to fuck up.

I looked over, at the row of girls. Aliza and Caroline were both looking. Their faces were smeared blue. Their hair shined.

We reached the front and looked down. It was such a light piece of wood – almost blonde-colored. Next to us were Mo's uncles and some close family friends we didn't know. The rabbi ran a hand through his beard and looked into Vern's eyes.

"Now, remember, boys, to lift from the knees. And be careful when you load it into the back of the car. There's a lip there – you know – to prevent it from sliding around, so be sure when you're placing it down in the hearse that you go up and over."

Vern nodded. I looked back, over my shoulder. Mo's head was on his mother's neck.

"Okay," said a burly man in a blue suit. "You – take the front."

He was pointing to me.

I moved toward the front and Vern came with me. We all slid our fingers underneath the wood at the same time. The man to my left turned to me. "I hope I don't get a splinter."

---

[14] The Hebrew text in translation is: "O God, full of compassion, Thou who dwellest on high! Grant perfect rest beneath the sheltering wings of Thy presence..."

"One, two, three," the rabbi said. We lifted. It was dead weight in our hands. I felt a strain in my knees.

"Move!" barked the burly man. I began shuffling my feet toward the door. The rabbi scurried out from behind the procession. He opened the door and waved his hand at us, as if urging us through. Behind me I felt the weight of Mo's father lurching forward, inside the wooden slats. It was like having a great big breeze at my back while walking down the Alley's wind tunnel. "My fingers are slipping," Vern said.

"Noooo, Daddy, noooo!"

I looked back. Jacob was running after us, grabbing onto Vern's legs, shrieking.

"Jacob!"

His mother leaped from her chair. He moved ahead. He was now walking completely underneath his father's coffin.

"Jacob! Come back here this second!"

"No, Daddy, please! Please don't go. Please. I love you so much. I'll never do anything again. Ever. Please. *Daddy*. No. Nooooo!"

Everyone in the funeral parlor gasped. A wail went up from the women's section, particularly Aliza and Caroline's row.

"Daddy, daddy!"

He extended his hand — and caressed the bottom of the coffin.

"Nooo! You can't take him. He's mine!"

We kept walking forward. He reached again to hold onto the coffin, which was passing him. He missed and fell and landed on his face. We were already at the door.

I turned back to see his mother scoop him up, clutch him against her breast and faint, on the spot, onto the floor.

****

We went through the door. There was another short hallway. I kept walking. The rabbi again got in front of us. He approached the far wall and pulled a handle I hadn't seen. A door opened and the outside light spilled in. It was bright. We walked through. There was a pain in my bent fingers – radiating out from the knuckles. It was problematic that the bottom was straight instead of round. You couldn't grip it. Below us was a flight of stairs and a black Cadillac with a large rump.

"Be careful of the stairs," the rabbi said.

We tiptoed down, one by one.

"Oh," said the driver, an older man in a black suit and cap. He had been reading a paper. He threw the newsprint to the floor and grabbed a handle on the back of the car. Two vertical doors popped open. We bent from the knees and thrust the coffin forward – and up.

****

Vern lifted the backwards shovel and drove it hard into the half-wet earth.

It sounded like a man punching a bag of sand. I watched him. Then I did it. Then I watched him again.[15]

It took us 47 minutes to fill the hole in which Mo's father rested. Initially the clumps of dirt made pebble-like sounds against the coffin. But then, once a layer of dirt covered that wood, there was just the soft sound of like things being combined.

****

---

[15] At my father's funeral all of the men took turns shoveling in the dirt – that's how it's done in Judaism – only you have to shovel at first with the shovel backwards, to signal you don't want the person to go so quickly and then with the shovel forward, to signal you're moving on. By the way, Jeremiah doesn't say this, but I saw him bend over and cry into the mud by the grave. I'll never forget it.

We stood in the parking lot. The soft light of the breezy morning was on our faces. I picked up the plastic, two-handled cup and undid the knob which the building probably used for hoses. The water gushed out.

"So we have to wash now?" Caroline said.

"Well, I have to," I said. "I mean, you're not Jewish. You can do whatever you want."

"No, I'll do it."

I filled the cup and poured it over both hands. I looked around.

No towel. I wiped them against the inside of my jacket. I needed a shower and a blanket.

"Here," I said and gave her the cup.

She filled it. She splashed a tiny bit on her left hand, and then a tiny bit on her right. She looked at me.

"No towel?"

"I guess not."

"Okay."

She shook her hands out and the water droplets flew across the cemetery parking lot.

"What now?" she asked.

I shook my head.

"Caroline…"

"Yes?"

"Why in the world are you here?"

She walked away from me, toward a Camry parked two rows away. I thought she'd turn around. She kept going. I ran ahead.

"Hey – I only asked a question. What's going on here?"

She turned around swiftly. Her face was puckered.

"You shouldn't have asked."

"Why?"

"Because you don't want to know."

"Don't want to know what?"

She looked me straight in the eyes.

"We hooked up, okay? Freshman year. I mean, when you two were freshmen…For a few months."

"Are you serious? You hooked up with Mo?"

"Yes. That's what I said."

She looked away. I stepped back. My face was flushed. I was so embarrassed. And angry – really angry. And damn it – Shani had been right. Mo had cheated on Rosie.

"What the fuck! Did you feel you had to hook up with every young Jewish boy? Was that, like, your thing?"

"I guess it was," Caroline said. She walked up to me and she kissed my cheek. I tingled all over. She was so sensual.

"The little WASP girl needs her neurotic Jew. *Still.*"

Nov. 5, 2007

The events of the months after Mo's father's funeral seem to me related to the death. I don't how exactly. But there was an influence. Vern still spent all his time reading, but it seemed like he did it in a sad way now. There was a difference. Now that her magazine had folded, Shani studied a lot and took six classes a semester. Rosie felt a little threatened by this because she had always been the better student of the two of them. I never saw Aliza and I never saw Mo. I was glad about that and I hated it.

Also, since the funeral, Caroline had been sending me (dirty) text messages:

One day I went down to the river because I was lonely. I found a little hotel nearby and sat in the lobby. It was late.

I looked.

The sky had the yellowish blaze of a Turner. The tall reeds, of varying length, were like matchsticks against the setting sun. A broad area of water narrowed in the distance, a puddle turning into a ribbon.

The scene pressed upon me a sense of loneliness. I pulled my cell phone from my pocket and laid it on the radiator beneath the window. The screen was dark. I looked at it expectantly, as though it might at any second alight with an incoming message or call. That it did not served only to reconfirm my most indulgent notions of victimhood: no one ever calls *me*; I never get messages; I must subside on porn.

It seemed ages ago that I had had a girlfriend, had gone out at night, had been swallowed by parties. Seemed ages ago I had had a roommate, had had a best friend, had been part of a group.

Seemed so very long ago that I had felt connected to any entity at all.

The chunky slab of plastic stirred.

I was momentarily displeased, denied even the pleasure of being sulky. But then I was curious.

I glanced over. It was from Caroline.

"Hey. How r u?"

"Okay. Tired."

"Yeah. Probably from all that sex you've been having, eh?"

"What?"

"Oh, c'mon. Don't be modest. *Stud.*"

"Are you drunk?"

Pause.

"Yes."

"Oh, geez. Just be careful, k?"

"K – just for you!"

Just then, a flock of crows appeared in the window. I watched them flap across the horizon, like eyebrows in various states of arching.

****

One day Caroline called me up with what she termed "wild news." She was moving back to Philadelphia for her job (some gig involving the administration of charter schools). Though I doubted she could have, I nevertheless wondered whether she hadn't requested the move – and whether I wasn't her reason. The thought troubled me, even though I found her wildly attractive. I needed to know about her time with Mo, but I also didn't want to hear the details.

****

The first thing I noticed was her brown leather riding boots. They had wooden soles and a few buckles and those straps on the side that help you pull them on. They rose up over her calves and covered her jeans.

"Give me a hug," Caroline said to me when she got closer. We were standing outside.

I leaned in and hugged her.

"It has been so long," she said.

"Not *that* long. I saw you at the funeral."

"Yeah."

We stepped away from each other, and I got a better shot of her. She was in a faded blue polo and a red cashmere sweater and her brown quilted jacket was tied around the hips. She looked ready to go fox-hunting.

"Where are we going to dinner?" she asked.

"I don't know,' I said.

"I forgot..." She brought a finger to her lips. "You keep kosher."

"Sorta."

She raised an eyebrow.

"Sorta?"

"Yeah. Dairy out is okay."

"Out?"

"I mean in restaurants."

"But not your apartment?"

"No."

"Hmm."

"Don't ask me to explain it...It's a weird Modern Orthodox thing."

"Can we eat at the Jewish Center?"

I was a little taken aback. She wanted to enter the heart of Jewville – where she'd probably feel a desperate need to be close to every guy.

"Sure," I said.

****

She saw me hesitate and frowned. Then she walked in herself. I followed but stopped when I realized I wasn't wearing a yarmulke. I had one in my pocket. I stuck my hand in, felt its smooth leather, and pulled my hand out.

I couldn't suddenly put it on.

She crossed the lobby quickly and got on the line to swipe a meal-card. I stood behind her and took mine out. Not having one, she snatched it from my hand.

"My treat," I said, though she had already taken it. The woman behind the desk swiped off two meals. Caroline and I proceeded to the food line. I bent down and grabbed us red trays from the counter.

She smiled. The bulges of her cheeks were perfectly round.

She took two slices of pizza and a piece of tilapia and I grabbed a tuna melt.

"Where should we sit?" she asked.

I looked out. All the tables were crowded. And the last thing I wanted was to be near any of my friends, including Aliza and Mo.

She pointed to the corner.

"Let's take that empty one, over there."

We sat. There was a moment of silence; neither of us knew where to begin.

"Where should I begin?" I asked.

"With your friends," she said.

"The plural isn't necessary."

"Very funny."

"No, really."

I took a bite of my tuna melt. A string of cheese dripped from the sandwich onto my lower lip. I let it dangle there, like the vine from which Tarzan swings. She picked at it with her finger and brought it to my lips. I kissed her finger.

"So what happened to all your friends? I saw them all at the funeral – your group, I mean."

"The gang was all there," I said.

"So?"

"So the gang's not much of a gang anymore outside of funerals."

"I see."

"Yeah."

She lowered a spoon into her mushroom barley soup and raised it up. The steam sea horses rose into her eyes.

"It's not like you used to date all those girls. I mean, Aliza – okay – I can understand why it'd be awkward around her. But what about the rest of the girls?"

I felt my chest tighten.

"How'd you know about Aliza?"

She snorted.

"C'mon, Jeremiah. What do you take me for? A hermit?"

"No, no, I don't. But let's be honest " – I waved my arms – "you're not exactly a part of this little world, are you? "

Her cheeks flushed. "No…"

"And it's not like you've been living around here or anything."

"True."

"So?"

She rolled her eyes.

"So…I have Facebook and Gmail and I speak to your friends more than you think."

I looked down and she seemed also to look away. Her words had come out wrong. But they made me think she was some sort of Jewish predator.

"If you really wanna know," I said.

"And I do—"

"I was close to Shani, but then I fucked up her magazine. She had a hearing and I vomited at it."

"Nice..."

"Yeah – it was a mess, I was a mess."

"But you're better now?"

"Sorta."

She nodded and lowered her spoon back into the soup. I ripped a piece of crust off my tuna melt and nibbled it.

"What about Rosie? Aren't you still friends with her?"

"I guess. But she's always running around. It's not like she's easy to talk to."

"There's Vern..."

"Yeah, there's Vern. He reads a lot, though..."

She nodded. I picked up my tuna melt and took a big bite. She tipped back the remainder of her soup into her mouth. Behind her, I saw a largish boy with dirty-blonde hair enter.

"Fuck," I mouthed. But it was audible.

"What?" She turned. Then she saw Mo walking over to us behind her.

"Oh."

"Yeah..."

She whipped her head back to the table and tossed her hair back.

"Don't make it out to be a big deal. It was three years ago..."

I frowned.

"You're uncomfortable, I can tell...Jeremiah, please...Don't be silly...I clearly don't like him anymore."

I shoved my food tray away from me, down the table, and rested my hands in front of me.

"I just need to know a few things – 'cause the whole thing's too weird."

"Okay..."

"How the hell did that start and how come I never saw you guys and why the fuck were you flirting with me when you were into him?"

I took a deep breath. My hands were shaking and my heart was pounding.

"I don't know when it started. I really don't. It was at the beginning of my senior year, and I think I met Mo when he dropped off his columns, and then we texted for awhile, but I don't know when it actually started. And you did actually see us, that day at the museum. I was there to meet Mo."

I couldn't believe that. She had been there that day to see him. I had thought the whole the time it was a coincidence.

"Why did you think I was in front of the same painting for at least an hour?" she asked.

"I'm an idiot," I said.

"You couldn't have known. And as for liking him, I don't know I ever did. But you were getting with Aliza. And I saw how close your whole group was. And I wanted in."

She sounded pathetic and sad.

"Oh, Caroline, that's ridiculous. You could've just hung out with us if you wanted to."

"I'm not sure about that. You were really tight-knit."

Just then Mo reached us.

"Hey," I said.

He didn't look at me but at Caroline.

"I didn't know you were gonna be here, Car."

She rubbed her left arm with her right and turned away.

"Yeah."

"You should've told me."

"It was last minute."

"No worries. Have a good time. We'll talk."

He looked down at her, smiled and walked away.

****

We walked under a canopy of trees. It was dark, and the branches from each side of the pavement were tangled above us. They looked like pubes.

We reached the shopping arcade west of campus. The restaurants and bars were filled with students. There was a buzz. Everyone was loud.

Caroline grinned.

"They're just trying to drown it out."

"Drown what out?"

"The sense they have. That the night will be disappointing."

I nodded. We crossed the street and kept walking. One block, then another. Finally:

"Here."

I looked up. It was an old row house, painted in pastels – pinks and blues. It looked totally out of place amongst the red brick of its neighbors.

"This is my new place."

She walked up the stairs to the door and slid in the key. There was a click and then another. She twisted the knob. "Damn – it's stuck." She lowered her shoulder and rammed ahead. The door gave way and she stumbled into the foyer.

"Tada!"

****

I lay on the queen-size bed, my arms stretched on either side of me. There was a slight creak and then she emerged from the closet. She was wearing a grey tank top and boy-short panties.

"What do you think?" she said.

"I think I'm hungry…"

She sashayed forward – a few steps and then a pause and then more steps. I stared at her through the space between my pecs. Finally she reached the foot of the bed.

"Ready?"

"For wha—"

Creak!

She landed on top of me, and the bed buckled.

"Uhhh…"

"Don't worry – that's normal. It always makes that sound."

"Uh, okay."

She crawled forward, on her hands and knees. I was now under her, her breasts dangling over me.

"And what," she asked, twirling a finger above my nose, "have you been up to sexually?"

I coughed.

"Uh….well…."

I felt something un-crinkle in my pants.

"Nothing. Just the usual doctor's appointments."

She slid her body upward, so that instead of looking at her face I now looked at her breasts. It was definitely moving.

I put my hand on the back of her neck and pulled her down. She giggled. She reached down and pulled her wife-beater up from her belly-button. I did the same with my t-shirt. Our skin touched.

She slid a hand into the circumference of my boxer's waistband. I wrapped my arm around her back and clasped her bra hooks between my middle finger and index. I pressed my thumb between the bra's two straps. *Click*. They fell away.

Her hand moved up my navel, past my chest, onto my neck.

I bridged my back and raised my hips. She let out a giggle, as though my pelvis were a feather, tickling her.

I thought for a moment – holy crap – I'm back on a bed with Caroline years after we first touched.

She lowered her lips. I opened. Our tongues met – hers was warm and tasted faintly of mushroom barley – and twirled. The skin on her neck, under my hand, pimpled. I pulled away and grabbed her shoulders and threw her to the bed. She was under me now, and I could see her smile and the brightness in her eyes, though they were closed. I rolled her arms to the sides of the bed and held them there with my own. She didn't offer resistance. Her body felt loose. I lowered my head onto her shoulder blade and pressed my lips onto the neck area just below her ear.

I just felt like sucking her away. Like she was a sexual milkshake. And then I saw it. And froze.

"Why'd you stop?" she said.

But I couldn't answer. I was staring at the pocket knife I had spotted on her dresser against the wall.

March 1, 2008

The light air wafted through the restaurant's open windows and door. It ruffled skirts and tousled hair and fell lightly on our necks, like a sun shower. It was a 60-degree March day and the perfect one on which to have a birthday party.

"Josh," I said, turning to him. "This is the perfect day on which to have a party."

"What an original sentiment," Shani said. She was still angry at me for having ruined the magazine hearing and now it was coming out at Josh's party.

Josh had invited the college gamut – from classical pianists to semi-Hasidic comedians. I turned to my right, where Rosie had quietly sat for the 20 or so minutes since we had arrived. She looked stunning – in a sad way. Her hair was a shimmering black and it fell along her cheeks and onto her shoulders like a silky tassel. She was in a red turtleneck; I felt somehow close to her.

"It feels kinda empty," I said, "doesn't it?"

She shook her head, as if waking up.

"Huh?"

"I mean, even with all these people, it seems empty. Like we don't belong."

"I guess. Where's Caroline?"

"You kidding? You know I couldn't tell Josh I'm dating a non-Jew."

"Makes sense."

"Where's Mo?"

She bit her lip. I realized suddenly they hadn't been dating for years.

"Not that we speak, but he's an *avel*[16]...he can't come to a party. You know that."

"I forgot. I'm sorry."

Around us, the festivity was now in full swing. A bottle of Jose Cuervo Silver was being passed around, and emptied, and so was a mug of limes. Also on the table were platters of hummus, tehina, babaganoush, pita, laffah, tabouleh, shakshuka, shish kabob, schnitzel and Moroccan cigars.

Rosie didn't eat a thing.

"I got to get Mo back," I said.

"Huh?"

"I see your empty plate. I also miss him."

She shook her head and blinked.

"I don't know what you're talking about, but I'd like it if you stopped."

"I goofed by bringing him up. But now that I have, I might as well take advantage of it."

She grabbed her napkin from the table and blew her nose.

"Okay."

"I just miss him."

She stared at me coldly.

"Why should *you* need him so badly?"

"Guys can be close."

She sniffed.

"You got Vern."

"It's not the same. Mo and I could talk."

Our table was really noisy now. All around us various small conversations were taking place. Moishe O'Reilly (a convert, clearly), had challenged Jim Dries to a falafel ball eat-off. One

---

[16] Mourner.

of said balls, having been smushed into Moishe's mouth belatedly, once their mutual friend Tim had called time, had, in accordance with that ruling, been spit out. It soared through the air – over the old fashioned glass Heinz bottle and the plastic squirter of hot sauce – and right into Shani's lap. "Ahh, gross!" she shrieked, jumping from her seat, so that the ball might plummet farther, onto the restaurant tiles.

I heard a sigh. I turned. Rosie's hand was on my own.

"I'm sorry I'm being so stubborn. Yeah, no – I know what you mean. You had something there – whatever. I get it."

"Yeah."

"You know what we need?"

I looked her in the eyes. They were as dark as her hair, and steely.

"What?"

"We need some way to show him he needs us, you know? Like something we do that other people don't."

"I've already tried. He thinks he doesn't need anything."

"Yeah."

I looked out over the table. Immediately I caught sight of Shani, who must've been staring at me. I felt my face tighten – and then, suddenly, relax. I had an idea.

"Stay here, okay? I'll be right back."

She scrunched up her face. I stood up and looked out. The table was packed and all down the line were bobbing heads. Some had the drunkard's droop.

I skirted past Simon – the lone male nursing student I knew – who had stumbled to the bathroom, and then Lauren, who was up ostensibly to get air (she was really on her way to sneak an outdoor smoke). Then I was there: behind Shani, whose head was bent forward, deep into a falafel.

"Hey," I said.

"What do you want?"

I patted her on the shoulder and, with a slight nudge, pushed her to the left. I sat.

"If you stay here," she said, "I'm getting up."

"I need to ask you a favor, and I hope you can forgive me."

She frowned.

"What?"

"It's not a big deal."

"Tell me."

"Vern gave you a key to the Zelosophic Society. He mentioned it once."

"So?"

"So Mo hates me right about now, and if you give me the key I can make it better."

"Is that so?"

"Yes. Nothing else will work. I even sent a hooker to his room once."

"What?"

"I was desperate."

She sniffed.

"I'm not going to give it to you. Even if I wanted to, I couldn't. I already lent it to someone."

I touched her shoulder.

"Here's the idea. I thought if I could find a book in the literary society that would make Mo happy, something really special, I could communicate how I feel and he would understand me."

"Ask Vern for *his* key."

"I can't. He would never go for it. He already told me never to speak about the place."

She put her finger to her lips.

"I change my mind. You should definitely go up there. One-hundred percent."

I frowned..

"Don't tease me. You don't even have the key."

"I don't, but if I had to guess, I'd say the person I lent it to left the door open. Just a guess."

She laughed and I was scared.

****

The air around us was like milk at the bottom of a cereal bowl – white, but with shades of blue and red and green. The light, such as it was, revealed small corners of the staircase – a cobweb here, a nicked tile.

"Maybe this wasn't such a good idea," I said.

"Oh, stop. We haven't even gotten there yet."

Rosie tossed her hands in the air and continued walking. One step, followed by another, and then a third. Our feet, in the damp well, sounded like marbles hitting a wood floor.

"I'm not made for this kind of climb," she said.

"That makes two of us, but remember, we're not doing it for us. We're doing it for him."

She turned back to me, looking down the black pit at the center of the spiraling steps.

"And who is that again?"

I smiled.

"The big doofus we both miss."

She sighed. "Right."

Finally the top landing came into view. It was a little patch of dusty floor adjacent to a large rope.

"What's that cord?" she asked.

"Don't touch it. I've been told it rings a bell."

"Really?"

She tiptoed up to it and squinted into its fibers.

"How loud do you think it would be, if pulled it?"

"Don't you dare. Pretty loud, though."

I grabbed her by the arm. "Okay, come with me. Now's the moment of truth." We approached the door at the end of the landing and I reached out. The knob felt loose. I gave it a little twist. The door receded.

"Nice."

I stepped back and she walked through. I followed. The College Hall hallway was deserted. There was a lone mop propped up against one of the painted portraits of the college founders – and, for some reason, a red cardigan was slung from it.

"Seems like the custodian's getting down."

She rolled her eyes.

We walked ahead. I turned.

"Here's the door," I said. "*You* open it."

She recoiled.

"Why me?"

"You have the feminine touch."

She folded her arms across her chest. "Don't be a pussy. Either we're gonna get in trouble or it won't be open it at all. Now just turn it."

"Okay."

I reached for the knob. It felt insecure. I pulled. The door came with me.

"Yes."

She smiled. "Alright, let's do this thing." She stepped past me, into the stairwell. I followed. A faintish red light reached us from above. I looked up, but could only see the framed programs on the wall. She turned back.

"You're the one who's been here before. *You* lead."

I nodded. There was a slight creak. I jumped back.

"What the hell's wrong with you?" she said.

"You didn't hear that?"

"No."

She put one foot on the first stair and pushed off. Then she was in motion. I did what she did. My legs felt leaden.

Creak.

She stopped.

"I heard *that.*"

"See!"

She started breathing hard. She brought her left hand to her chest.

"Okay. Nothing to be worried about. It's probably just the building."

I nodded.

"Yeah. It's old."

She put two fingers across her left wrist.

"Still…my heart…it's racing."

"It's from all that fucking caffeine you have."

"Not now, J. This isn't the time."

"*Fine.*"

She resumed climbing. I followed. She reached the top and froze.

I stared up at her, also still.

"What is it?"

"I just heard something else…A voice."

"You sure?"

"I think so."

I gulped. Her eyes were wide open and her hand was back on her chest.

"I feel tight," she said.

"What?"

"My chest. It feels tight."

I rolled my eyes.

"Jesus, Rosie. I'm sure you're fine. You just drink too much coffee. Now…what are we gonna do? Do you think we should leave?"

"I dunno."

"'Cause I'm a little scared."

"Me, too."

We both leaned forward, as if trying to listen more closely.

"I don't hear anything," I said.

"Neither do I."

I nodded.

"Should we proceed?"

"Yeah. What's the worse that can happen?"

"A janitor cuts our balls off."

"But I don't have balls."

"True. You go first…"

She turned back at me, her eyes like daggers.

"I will. But you owe me."

She tiptoed out, across the carpet, and down the hall. I followed behind her. Her butt wriggled cutely.

Creak.

She jerked around.

"What the fuck was that?"

"A creak."

"That's it. I'm out of here." She marched past me, back toward the staircase. I grabbed her arm..

"If you think I'm turning back after all of this, you're crazy. It's probably just the janitor having sex. We'll go past him, into the library."

"What? Are you mad?"

"No, I'm serious. He won't notice us. He's probably pleasuring a broom."

She pulled away from me. "You're sick. I'm out." She walked toward the stairs. I stared at the back of her head.

"If you leave now, you'll never get back with Mo."

She turned toward me.

"Fine. But you're really a bastard."

I nodded. I walked ahead, down the red-carpeted hallway with the yellowish lights and golden sconces. I couldn't see her, but I heard her behind me. I was at the door – of the library room – the one with the big wooden table on which Vern had a year before plopped down a big volume of Japanese novels and then, afterward, Egyptian inscriptions. I looked over my shoulder.

"This is it. Follow me."

I pushed against the heavy wood – which was carved with lions and eagles. It swung open as if it weighed nothing.

"Holy fuck!" I shouted.

"Jeremiah!" shouted Mo. "What are you doing here?!"

He was lying on top of Aliza, who was on top of the table on which Vern had plopped down two books. His maroon long-sleeve t-shirt was pulled up to his nipples and his bare stomach was pressed against hers. His lips were on her neck. She looked at me pleadingly, her chocolate eyes wide open – her body smothered by my former roommate's above her.

"Jeremiah!" she pleaded. "Why are you here?"

"I dunno," I said.

She bent her neck toward me, and her nose moved downward – like she were an Eskimo kissing. I leaned my own nose in and moved it upward. She made a whimpering sound.

Mo was just lying there – frozen. His shirt, still as high as his chest, looked like a brown paper bag pressed down around the neck of a beer.

"Oh my god!"

Rosie had walked in.

"Mo," she shrieked, "what the fuck? Is that – Aliza?"

Boom.

I turned back. Rosie was slumped against the wall, her hand clutching her chest.

"My heart!"

I rushed to her. So did Mo, who jumped off the table. I brushed her hand aside and placed my own on her left breast.

"Don't worry. You're just tense."

She pushed me off and slumped farther down. She clutched her chest.

"No, it hurts! I'm in pain!"

"How much caffeine have you had?" Mo shouted.

She shook her head and began to cry.

"I dunno, I dunno!"

He knocked me aside and shoved his hands into the pocket inside her cardigan.

"Caffeine strips!"

He held up six small pink packets against the room's light.

"What the hell are these?" I shouted.

"Caffeine strips," Mo said, "they're like Listerine strips, only soaked in caffeine."

"My fucking heart!"

She was shrieking now.

"I can't feel my arm!"

I looked at Mo.

"We need to get her to the hospital."

He nodded.

Aliza just laid there – her right nipple poking out from her plunging black v-neck – her eyes completely dark – set on me. I nodded at her. She blinked. A tear slid down her cheek.

"I'll grab her under this arm," Mo said, "you do the other."

"Right."

We hoisted Rosie from the ground.

"I'm gonna die!"

"You'll be okay," Mo said, "J – dial 911. *Now.*"

I shoved my hand into my pocket.

My phone was the only bulge.

****

The curtain ruffled. A man in green scrubs slid through. The white light on him revealed heavy bags. Rosie popped up in her bed. Mo and I leaned forward in our chairs.

"Well, Doc," she said. "How about it? Am I gonna be okay?"

He gave a half-smile.

"The good news is, you didn't have a heart attack."

"And the bad news?"

He opened his mouth, then closed it. He coughed.

"You gotta stay away from the caffeine. You're killing yourself…And you're gonna have to be here for awhile. We need to observe you."

****

I walked into the white light, near the elevators. Behind me was the persistent beat of the heart monitors: beep…beep…beep…

I felt Mo behind me. I spun.

"How could you?

"You're broken up. It's allowed."

"I still love her. You must know."

"Why must I? We don't talk."

"We would if it were up to me."

That would show him, I thought – how I care – how much I think about it.

"It's not always about you," he said. "You can't just write about people and you can't just stop them from going out."

"You're going out with her?"

He looked like he realized he had made a mistake and now he seemed bashful. He lowered his head. Then he nodded.

I was stunned. Not just because I knew she still loved me but because Mo didn't need anything. I couldn't understand how he could be with her.

"Did she make you do anything?" I asked. "Anything violent?"

He looked confused.

"No. Why would she?"

March 18, 2008

Caroline and I were sitting on her bed. It was a Friday afternoon.

"I want you to bring me to *shul*[17] tonight," she said.

I was totally taken aback. Why would she want to go there? Was she looking to see Mo?

"Why?" I asked.

"I want to *daven*[18]."

"Are you serious?"

"Do I sound it?"

"But Caroline, this is absurd. I don't even know if I buy into all that. In fact, I'm pretty sure I don't."

"It has great power."

"Great power? You're queen of the WASPs. Who taught you about this power? John Updike pretending to be Philip Roth?"

"I taught myself. I've been reading the *siddur*."[19]

I couldn't believe what I was hearing. My *shiksa* girlfriend was more familiar with "*Modeh Ani*"[20] than I was. This was getting really strange. It was like she was trying to take over the life I had had.

"How do you know you like this? You've never even lived it."

"I wish I had," she said. "You're so lucky – you got to grow up in a spiritual home with a real core. You got to take a day of rest every week and just meditate in the presence of God. Do you know how much of a difference that would've made for

---

[17] Synagogue.
[18] Pray.
[19] Prayer book.
[20] This is the first prayer a person recites upon waking and literally means, "Thankful am I."

me? I could've used that in my childhood and now I'm really far behind because I never did it. But I'm figuring it all out. Your friend Josh has been showing me things in the *Beit Midrash.*" [21]

Josh – so he was behind this!

"Is he brainwashing you?"

She looked offended.

"He's *enlightening* me, Jeremiah. Don't be rude."

She was right – I was blowing my chances at getting head.

"I'm sorry. We'll talk about this another time. Now, on to more important things."

I cupped her right breast and moved in to kiss her. She pulled away.

"I don't think we should," she said.

"Why?" I asked, but I already knew what was coming.

"I've been thinking about it," she said, "and we should probably be *shomrei negiah.*" [22]

---

[21] This means "House of Study" and refers to a library filled with Judaica on the third floor of the Jewish Center.

[22] This means Jeremiah got screwed and his girlfriend now wanted to observe the prohibition against touching the other sex.

Senior Year

Sept. 5, 2008

"Tickets?" the conductor asked.

"Here."

He pulled the light-blue paper from my hand. He squinted.

"No, you need to sign it. Here."

He handed me a pen and the ticket. I took them and leant over the fold-down tray in front of me. I pressed down with the inky point. My "J" was big and looping.

"Here," I said.

"Thanks."

The air in the train cabin was hot and stuffy – the air of summer.

In two more hours I'd be on campus. A move-in by train. Where were my parents? What happened to that Mets game? When everything came into focus through the binoculars?

It seemed like so long ago that I had bought my supplies at Bed Bath & Beyond.

Nov. 28, 2008

"It won't get hard."

Caroline looked up at me, from the point of my open fly. I stared down my somewhat hairy chest.

"Here – try this." I reached down and placed my left hand above my dick and my right hand below it. I opened the latter palm and slid it up and down – as though it were a sander.

"Are you sure? That looks painful."

"Of course, I'm sure. It's *my* penis."

"Okay."

She bent down, her long hair covering her face. Somewhere beneath all that shimmering black was her pearl necklace.

"Still nothing."

"I know why you can't get hard."

I grabbed a pillow and put it over my face.

"I don't want to hear this again."

"It's true – you know it's true. That's why you don't want to hear it."

"I like *you*."

She grabbed her sweater from the side of the bed.

"Clearly not enough."

Dec. 15, 2008

I slouched in my desk chair, my pelvis inflected upward.

My arm was extended toward the wobbly member hanging from my open fly, which was like the trunk of a microscopic elephant. I typed in the address of the search engine – the one I use for these pursuits alone, with the history tracker turned off. I thought hard for a moment, trying to conjure a search term I hadn't recently used.

"College," I typed. Then, pausing, I reconsidered.

"Nipples," I added.

The video results were not promising. One seemed to be an educational film on breastfeeding for teenage mothers. Another, starring a lascivious mosquito prone to biting plaid-skirted adolescents, was animated and in Japanese.

Moving my hand from the pinkish appendage to the silver laptop, I clicked on the search box again.

"Hot college nude," I typed, making sure to retain the academic term, so as to seem natural and healthy, interested in my peers alone – and not base perversity.

"Sluts," I added, just to be safe.

The first video seemed suitable. The still shot showed an auburn girl, legs spread as in a Courbet, a copy of *The Way We Live Now* covering her muff.

I turned up the computer's volume – not worried about my neighbors, the headphones being plugged in – and clicked.

The girl – Rosa, apparently – was leaning against a pillow on the bed. Her interlocutor, an off-screen man I imagined resembled Tom Selleck, asked about her favorite books. Somehow, the proper response to this question, instead of requiring words, involved the removal of her bra and panties.

An autoerotic act, hinging on the manipulation of labia, was performed, followed by the insertion of a neon green toy.

I stroked myself vigorously. And in the flush of excitement, all worldly concern dissipated. No longer did I recall the mistakes I had made, or the karmic ways I had been punished for them. The wreckage of relationships receded, and all I could comprehend played out on the screen, in the vicinity of a moist ellipse.

DING

I was jostled to my senses by the ringing in my ear. A box popped up on my computer. It said I had a new email. I clicked. It was from the Jewish Center listserv.

"Congratulations to Mo Gross and Aliza Zuckerman on their engagement," it read. "We hope they build a *bayit ne'eman b'Yisroel*."[23]

The blood fled my penis like a peasant from Chernobyl.

---

[23] What you commonly wish an engaged couple – that they build a faithful/truthful house in the nation of Israel.

Dec. 16, 2008

The light slanted unevenly across the water.

Caroline's feet dangled over the railing, above the river. Mine, too.

"Do you think," she said, smirking (but it was not her usual smirk — more like a mask), "I should be upset that you care?"

"Don't give me that look."

She scowled.

Turning away from each other, we gazed at the water. There was a racing shell in the distance, hurtling toward us.

"It doesn't bother *me*," she said, "to know how you feel. But you talk about it. How rude is *that?*"

"I don't know what to tell you."

"I don't need to put up with this."

Her voice rose a pitch.

"I'm 24, I'm smart, I'm successful..."

She blinked repeatedly.

"I can't do it, I just can't, I won't..."

I felt the awkwardness of an onlooker.

"I – I – I..."

She let her head fall into her lap. She sobbed.

"And Aliza...Why do you care so much about her?"

I looked away.

"There will be many Orthodox guys who want me when I finish the conversion."

Jan. 20, 2009

"Honestly, J – I just don't get it. It doesn't make any sense to me."

He pivoted in air, so that he was now facing the mirror. The rope just barely slid under his Reeboks.

"I never said it made sense, Vern. I just couldn't help it."

He snorted.

"You couldn't help shooing away a beautiful older girl...That's retarded."

"Gimme that."

I grabbed the rope from his hands. I transferred the right handle to my right hand and began flicking it. The rope hit my laces.

"You suck."

"Fuck you."

I jumped off the ground and whooshed it twice beneath me.

"Take that! A double jump!"

"It didn't have to be like this...You could've put up a fight..."

Through the rope his face flickered – like an old silent movie.

"And what would be the point of that? I'd wind up letting her know I liked Aliza ...and even if I kept it a secret, so? Who cares? I'd still like her less..."

Vern held up an open hand.

"If you're not with the one you love..."

Feb. 14, 2009

"You're really smoking now."

I looked up at Hutchinson – at his white tufted hair and benevolent eye wrinkles.

"You mean that?"

"You know I do, Jeremiah. Look at this stuff." He grabbed a pile of papers from his desk. "It's sharp, funny." He waved it. "Hell, it even feels tight."

"Thanks."

"Do you have any idea how much progress you've made from when we first started? You were practically hitting me over the head with your description. And now you're just letting scenes play out."

"Thanks."

"*Still*, though, for all the talent I see, I'm not sure you know what you're doing."

"Huh?"

"I don't see a purpose in any of the vignettes. You don't seem to know why you're doing them. What the main reason is."

Of course, he was right. I realized it as he said it. The only writing that mattered was the stuff I did to show how I feel. Those other 36 people in the Quad – I had nothing to tell them.

"I'll be honest," he said. "I don't think you're ready for a project like this yet. You need to get your house in order first. You need to figure out why you care about these people in the first place."

I was stung – I had really wanted him to see my talent and promote me to his people and have his people promote me to the publishers. And I had wanted to climb up that fucking ladder and become known. But now all I could say was:

"When you've never had something before, do you think you're at all able to understand why you want it?"

March 7, 2009

Rosie picked up her tray and dumped its contents on my head.

"Holy fuck – that's cold!"

The ice cubes slid down my back, as well as a slice of lasagna.

"It should be," she said. "I told them specifically not to heat it."

"You're nuts," I said.

"She's nuts," Shani said.

"Nuts," Rosie said, "or drunk?"

"What's the difference?" I asked.

"The difference is that we're seniors. Intoxicated is not just not crazy, it's *mandatory*."

"True."

Shani bent down to pick up a slice of cheese that had fallen onto the Jewish Center floor.

"Man," she said, "you really got food everywhere."

Rosie nodded. She had been caffeine-free for months now and was delighting in those substances she *was* allowed.

"We *are* seniors," I said, looking out onto the sandy volleyball court beyond the Jewish Center. "We should *all* be like this."

Of course, I didn't feel happy.

Shani glanced down at her laptop, which was positioned to the side of her lunch tray. "Yeah, if it were only that easy…"

Rosie put her arm around her.

"Aww…is my pure BFF tired? Is she upset because she has a job with People already and the rest of us are unemployed?"

Shani brushed off Rosie's arm.

"Hey, it's not funny. It's really hard work…They already have me tracking people."

"Aww, poor thing."

Rosie stuck her tongue out. Shani grabbed an ice cube from her Styrofoam cup of soda and placed it on that tongue.

"Take that."

"Soo," I said, sticking my arm between them. "Are you two going to the engagement party?"

They looked at each other and then me.

"Um…er…"

"You can say yes. *I'm* going, after all."

"You are?" Shani was louder than she had intended.

"Shh!" Rosie said.

"How could I not go?" I said.

"I can think of lots of reasons," Shani said.

"These are my *first* friends to be married," I said, "even if I am estranged from one and infatuated with the other."

"Which is which?" Rosie asked. Shani was shoving her hand in her bag – trying, it seemed, to bury something deep inside.

"What are you doing?" I asked. She whipped around.

"Nothing," she said. "They are the first ones to be married. They get some kind of medal for that, don't they?"

April 8, 2009

"What are your plans for after graduation?" asked Mrs. Stern, a frizzy-haired woman, leaning into the table, over the bowl of charoset on the *seder* plate.[24]

"I want to write," I said.

"And do you have a job for that?"

"No."

"In my day," said Mr. Stern , "the main journalistic outlet was The Saturday Evening Post. I remember, I used to read it when I came home from school. Always with a Norman Rockwell on the cover. And the articles? They were excellent. Always. You just don't get that quality anymore."

"What are you talking about?" His wife grabbed his wrist. "You grew up in the '70s. The Post wasn't even around."

Mr. Stern adjusted his glasses.

"No – I'm quite sure I read it in the '70s, after school. I'd unwrap a Twix and pour a glass of milk."

"Impossible! Twix wasn't introduced until the '80s."

Mr. Stern went quiet.

My parents, who had watched the Sterns, turned to me. My dad gripped his knife. It was a knife, and I thought of her.

"Tell me where you've applied," he said.

"It's been mostly internships."

"Where?"

"Magazines and newspapers."

"Name some."

"I applied to all the Hearst magazines. And Conde Nast's."

My father frowned.

"Do they pay?"

---

[24] The ritual plate at the center of the Passover Seder, which contains a hard-boiled egg, a shank bone, *charoset* and some other things.

"Some, but very little."

"Hmm."

He took the napkin from his lap, refolded it on the diagonal and re-placed it. My mom, though silent, continued staring. Her brown eyes were bigger than usual, her cheeks redder and her lips more curled.

"If they don't pay, shouldn't you consider a real job?" asked my dad.

"There are none. No one's hiring. Most places are cutting."

He shook his head.

"It's time for you to consider non-writing jobs."

"Is this really the time…?"

"It's April, Jeremiah! It's long past the time."

April 18, 2009

The light filtered meekly through the grimy window. Vern's head was deep inside a book.

"C'mon, Vern – you can't spend the entire time reading – it's rude. Aren't you gonna ask me how my Passover was?"

He didn't look up.

"How was your Passover?" he asked.

"Shitty – it was very shitty."

"Sorry to hear it." His nose was still an inch away from a line of text about Ayurvedic medicine.

"Talk to me."

He leaned back.

"Alright."

"Tell me about Arizona – wasn't Shani also there for Pesach?"

"Yes…"

"Did you guys spend the whole time together?"

"Yes."

Gosh, it was odd that they had made it so long while my relationships had failed.

"I still have the hardest time imagining you guys together," I said.

Vern bent over and took a look into his backpack, which was by his knees, under the desk.

"Let's forget about it," he said, "k?"

"I didn't know the topic bothered you."

I brought up the subject of jobs and he told me Shani had been hired by People, which I already knew, and that Rosie had been hired by Dunkin Donuts' marketing team to come up with promotions for its new coffee-based drinks. Mo, apparently, was heading to The Atlantic in Washington for a six-month paid internship (Hutchinson had landed him the job, Vern said, which was weird because I hadn't known Hutchinson was even working with Mo; I thought that was just me, and he hadn't gotten me anything).

"What about you?" I asked him.

"I'm not leaving," he said.

"You're not graduating?"

"No, I am. But the Zelosophic Society has a curatorial position. Basically, every couple of years they hire someone to look after the place – someone to study in the library and create the right atmosphere and also to plan lectures and events."

"What does that mean for you and Shani? Are you guys gonna stay together?"

He took a deep breath.

"We don't really have a choice."

I didn't know what he meant.

"We're married, Jeremiah."

"Holy shit!"

He smiled. "I know…wait…I'll show you." He dug into his backpack and removed a gold band.

"Check this out…"

I held up my hands. "I'm speechless," I said. And I really was.

"I'll do the talking. We were both in Arizona for *Pesach*[25], right? Well, a couple months ago, Shani and I were talking about getting married – 'cause we'd been doing that a lot – and it kinda seemed almost a matter of time – and I said to her, 'We're gonna have to invite a ton of people – because you know just about everyone.' And she blanched and looked at me

---

[25] Passover.

and started to cry. And I asked her what was wrong and she said, 'Oh, god. I don't want everyone at our wedding.' And I asked, 'Why? They're your friends.' And – get ready – she said to me, 'All those people – they're just gossips. I wanna have a private moment.'"

"That's the funniest thing I've ever heard."

"I know. I love her, so I listened. Besides, I enjoy privacy...We hatched this plan that, since we're both gonna be in Arizona, one day, we'll get a car and drive to Vegas and get married...We had an excuse to tell our parents for where we were and everything – and on the set day we got in this old Lumina we borrowed from friends who had moved out to Scottsdale and we drove up and got married."

I leaned against the bookcase. I was feeling very weak suddenly. He was gonna be married and Mo was gonna be married[26] and I was alone and one ex was now a convert and the other was a backstabber (and wanted me to stab myself – though I still loved her).

"Don't get me wrong," Vern said, "we didn't tell anyone and we're still gonna have a big Jewish wedding with all the guests. We just figured you only get one chance to come together the first time...we might as well do it alone."

---

[26] Incidentally, these early marriages are very common in the Modern Orthodox community, which has trended rightward (that is, toward more religiosity) in the last few decades.

April 25, 2009

I knew I shouldn't do it as I hopped in the car. As I breathed the hot air that smelled like the plastic dashboard. But I had to. I had questions.

It took me two and a half hours to get to Long Island. Then I was in front of the house – a ranch with a bay window in the front, a bare tree and a faded lawn.

I walked slowly from the car to the door. I felt the stones in the walkway wobble beneath me.

I pressed the buzzer. Nothing. I knocked. Still nothing. I used the metal knocker on the door. A clanging noise.

The door whooshed open.

It was the tall, grave man. I recognized him from the winter's day.

"Who are you?"

"I'm Jeremiah. I just have a few questions about Aliza. I really need to know—."

He frowned.

"I'm afraid you have the wrong house."

"Oh."

I looked at him.

We stood there for several seconds – our eyes locked.

And then:

"You mean Rhoda. Come in."

He led me through the foyer and the dining room. On the cabinets were pictures of Aliza and this man – who was tall and bald and had a grey beard. He was hugging her on a ski slope; she was hanging from his broad shoulders in a swimming pool (she must've been 16 in that one; I could tell because she was wearing a halter-top bikini and her breasts were obviously formed – they looked like they do now, downward sloping, but not in a droopy way but with insouciance, as if saying, yeah, we're here, you want this? – and I thought, Wow, her breasts are just hanging down there, on his back); in a third picture, the two of them were sitting cheek to cheek in a wicker chair on a porch – the sun was setting. She looked to be 11.

We sat on a beaten-up couch.

"I'm sorry about that," he said. "I still think of her as Rhoda."

"Aliza's not her name?"

"No." He cracked his knuckles. He seemed unsure about continuing. "She started calling herself that in high school."

"Oh."

"After her mother left."

"I didn't know—"

"She got more religious then. Started going to temple."

That must've been hard, I said, the mother leaving. He said, On part of the family. I asked what he meant. He said, She took my younger daughter with her – Kaitlin. She was 8 at the time. Aliza was 12. I gestured to the pictures on the countertops of him and his older girl.

"That explains why you're so close," I said.

"Not exactly," he said.

May 1, 2009

I dreamt last night of graduation:

There we sat, side by side, in the wide-open bowl of the brick stadium, with the sun beating down on our exposed necks. The rays of light fell everywhere – so diffuse as to lend the entire green field of artificial turf a sacred-seeming gleam, to make the entire long, metal bleachers glint, to bathe the stage in a blinding whiteness. Every surface I touched, even my chair, had a baked quality. It was stuffy as hell underneath my synthetic gown, and madly did I want to tear it off and scratch – to dig my nails into small of my back and claw away at the flesh. The heat was radiant and convecting, rising from the rows of graduates at the bottom of the stadium up to the stands and then falling again, like crackling firecrackers, the kinds that look like spiders when they descend, or an Alexander Calder mobile, onto our mortarboards.

Mo was to my right, his hands restlessly tapping away at his knees. The school president was speaking on the stage. I think she was making a joke about lawyers.

"This is it," I said.

"The end," he said.

"Just like, 'It is Clarissa…for there she was.'"

"'Like the descent of their last end, upon all the living and the dead.'"

"'Isn't it pretty to think so?'"

A moment passed.

"Oh, fuck," he said. "I can't think of anymore. Can you skip me one turn?"

"Fine. But you definitely know this one – from high school, at least. 'So we beat on, boats against the current, borne back ceaselessly into the past.'"

"Ummmm. Oh, shit, I can hear this one ringing in the back of my head. It's on the tip of my tongue…Errrr, 'Gatsby'?"

"Correctamundo."

"Oh, *I* got one now! Ready? 'He loved Big Brother.'"

"Aww, no way. That doesn't count."

"Why?"

"Cause, no offense to Orwell, but it's too easy to remember. Too simple."

"Who says they have to be complex?"

"I mean, compare it to this one. But first, close your eyes – it will heighten the effect."

Mo shook his head, as if to say, like Kel Mitchell, "Aw, here he goes again, with another of his crazy schemes."

"If you say so."

He shut his eyes, then blinked them a few times. Then his features went calm.

"Okay, good. Here it goes. 'And first I put my arms around him yes and drew him down to me so he could feel my breasts all perfume yes and his heart was going like mad and yes I said yes I will Yes.'"

Mo started from his seat as though shaken by a tremendous gust of wind.

"Now how in the hell did you memorize that?!"

I laughed. I grabbed the copy of *Ulysses* from beneath my seat.

"It wasn't so hard."

He smirked.

"You brought a book to your own graduation!?"

"Oh, c'mon. Do you realize how long the president has been going on for? What was I supposed to do? Just be her captive?"

"You could talk to me."

"*Ahh* – the choice from time immemorial. To converse or read. You really think you can match Joyce word for word?" He snatched my cap from me by its dangling tassel and twirled it in the air.

"Don't think I can. But can Joyce match me for being alive?"

May 2, 2009

Vern kicked up a clump of dirt with his Rod Lavers. It fell down, onto his shoe, and the nearby water, like sprinkles on a donut. He looked at me.

"That's one weirdass dream, J."

"I know."

"What are you gonna do?"

"I'm gonna go to the party."

He nodded.

"Your subconscious was telling you something."

"Oh, great."

He stroked his chin. "You need some plan. Something to say to Mo and Aliza – before it's too late…"

"I've already tried everything. And besides…I'm not gonna ruin their party …"

He sniffed. "You don't have to do *that*…"

"What else is there?"

He placed both hands on my shoulders.

"This is what you do. Get your journal—"

"Hey – how'd you know about that?"

"—print it out – twice. The whole thing – starting from the beginning of college…Put the copies in two boxes …Bring the boxes, in a bag, to the party…"

"You're insane."

"This is the tough part…When you see Mo and Aliza go off to a room— and they will, 'cause engaged couples always do, follow them and give them the boxes."

"I can't believe you're saying this…"

"Don't say anything. That's the most important thing. Don't say a word. Just leave the boxes."

I shook my head. "This is the craziest thing I've ever heard."

"Are you gonna do it?"

"Vern, you're my guru. Of course I'm gonna do it."

May 3, 2009

The engagement party in Vern's off-campus house was like a living, breathing thing; the old wooden colonial seemed to expand and contract: to suck in the light spring air from the sidewalk and belch out, in rhythmic spurts, that same air, but hotter, and heavier, thick with whiskey and facial oil.

Jeremiah walked into the room with a messenger bag over his shoulder. I was busy making conversation with the rabbi, but I saw him. He found an open space against a wall and put the bag down against it. Then he leaned back, his hands in his pockets.

The crowd in the middle of the room moved to the sides. Vern and Shani and Rosie shoved a glass coffee table to the wall. He started from his spot, then fell back.

The *simcha* dancing began slowly. The girls were on the far side of the room. At first, I fell into the circle with everyone else, and we went around singing *"Od yishama."* Then my brother, who had come for the weekend, grabbed me to form a smaller circle. We kicked our legs in opposite directions – as though warming up for field goals – and crossed our arms like pretzels. Vern joined us, and then Josh.

Someone jumped into the circle with shots of whiskey. We grabbed them and drank.

Around and around we went. The redness rose into our cheeks, the sweat spouted from our foreheads. From our foreheads, as condensation on a window. Our hands on each other's shoulders, our voices running hoarse, the lyrics repeated with a dizzying lilt: *Yet again will be heard in the hills of Judea, and the skirts of Jerusalem, sound of gladness and sound of happiness, voice of the groom and voice of the bride.*

"Come Jeremiah, join in!" someone shouted.

"Yeah," said another, "we need you here!"

He took a step forward, and then fell back again. A girl near him poured him a shot of vodka. He downed it.

"It's not right," someone said (I could read his lips). He wheeled around. It was Vern. He was in an unlined khaki blazer that pinched around the shoulders.

"This is Mo's day. Suck it up."

Jeremiah nodded.

"Here," Vern said.

He took the shot and downed it. Vern patted him on the back and they walked to the circle. He remained quiet at first, walking around stiffly. But slowly he gave in; he sang himself hoarse, he shuffled his feet, he smacked guys on their shoulders.

"Yet again will be heard in the hills of Judea, and the skirts of Jerusalem, sound of gladness and sound of happiness, voice of the groom and voice of the bride."

Josh left to pour more shots. I took advantage of the momentary break to thank him for coming. It wasn't much, what I said – something like, "It means a lot."

Josh returned with four shots. We downed them.

Vern draped his arm around me. Josh shook my hand. I excused myself – and walked to the girl's circle.

"Hey, Aliza – can I talk to your for a sec?...I could use a break." She nodded and followed me – up the staircase behind her, and onto the mezzanine level – a sort of balcony Vern's house has which is its best feature.

"Where are we going?"

I turned back to her.

"Just into a bedroom – to get some air."

We walked down the hallway and turned.

"I think this is Vern's room."

I knocked on the door and nothing happened.

"Alright…in we go."

The room was empty and cold. There was nothing in it but a small desk and bed.

"Spare," she said, behind me.

She put a hand on the bed and bent over. With the other hand she knocked off one heel, then another.

"My feet are killing me."

She hopped on the bed. I took off my jacket and laid it over his desk.

"Make room for me." I hopped on and the bed catapulted her onto me.

"That was convenient!" I said.

She smiled and curled into me. I asked the question I'd been meaning to ask for awhile.

"Aliza," I said. "Awhile back Jeremiah said something weird to me. Something I need you to clarify."

"Shoot."

"He asked me – this is hard to put. Basically, he asked me whether you had ever wanted me to be violent. Now, I know Jeremiah has his issues, but I don't think he would make that up."

She nodded. "He didn't."

"So what was he talking about?"

She sighed. "It doesn't matter, k?" She smiled. "I don't need that from you. That level."

"Level of what?"

"Passion."

Creak.

I turned. Jeremiah was in the doorway. That bag was over his shoulder.

"J, what are you doing here?"

He didn't say anything – just looked into my eyes and then Aliza's. I turned to her, over my shoulder. Her eyes were fixed on his.

"What's going on here?"

He walked over to the desk and placed the bag on top of it. He leaned in and unbuckled its two straps. He put his hands inside and removed two small cardboard boxes. He looked back at me, smiled – as if unable to speak – and placed the boxes on the desk.

"J, what the hell are you doing? What's inside those boxes?"

He sprung up – as if something had gone off within him – and turned around.

"They're...my..."

He looked at Aliza.

"Jeremiah!" she shouted. "What's going on?"

"Those boxes...They're stories" – he glanced down at Aliza and then at me – "about you."

"What?"

"I wrote these stories about you."

"What!" I banged the wall. "You fucking wrote about me again?"

"You don't understand. This is...my journal..."

"Get that outta here..."

He turned from me, to Aliza.

"Aliza...I love you...I did when we were freshmen, and I still do...Nothing that's come in the middle has mattered ...Here is my knife. Each page you read will plunge it deeper inside me."

I stepped to him.

"Get out of here," I said.

"And you, Mo…"

His voice was gentle.

"I love you, too…I dunno how else to say it…I guess you'll see …when you told me stories I felt it was right. You and Hannah looking up at the stars. That was *true*."

"You put that down?!"

I shoved him. He fell backwards, over the desk.

"Mo!" Aliza shouted. "Don't touch him!"

"You fucking wrote about me!" I screamed. He was behind the desk – in the little area between it and the wall.

He looked up, his eyes red.

"No." He trembled. "You don't understand."

"Oh, I fucking understand." I grabbed one of the boxes from the table. "I understand that you can't help yourself. That you have to use your friends as material…"

"Mo, no!" Aliza said. "Put that down!"

"Well, fine. If that's how you want it, that's how it'll be." I waved the box in the air. "You want everyone to read about me?" I looked back at Aliza – she was curled up in a ball, on the bed, shaking. I looked down on him. "You want everyone to read about *her*? This girl you supposedly love?"

"Mo, stop…please!"

"Well, fine…that's exactly what will happen, then, *okay*? Exactly what you'll get."

I took off – through the room, out the door.

"Mo – wait!"

I ran down the hallway, clutching the box against my chest. I felt and heard his steps behind me. In the distance I saw the banister of the mezzanine. Then I was a few feet away. Below me, through the balustrades, I could see all of the people. I reached forward and—

BOOM.

I felt pushed from behind and crashed to the floor. The box went flying from my hands, over the railing. A body – Jeremiah's – followed. I watched them float through the air – a boy and his words, borne along, for a single moment – like a calabash that drifts downstream.

His momentum carried him forward, his head pointed down. Then he was out of view.

CRACK.

I heard people gasp. My face was in the carpet. I sprung to my feet and ran onto the stairs. I tumbled. There was a ring of people in the middle of the living room.

"Excuse me!" I screamed, pushing through. There was one layer, then another and then a third. I reached the middle. It was totally dark. He was lying on his back, his head tilted upward, his arms at his sides, the floor scattered with paper.

"Jeremiah!! Are you okay?"

I flung myself onto him. He was looking up. His face was white, his eyes blank. A small trickle of blood flowed from his left ear.

"Oh, god, oh god! Get a doctor!"

I looked up, at all the faces.

"Someone *please* get a doctor!"

"Mo?"

The voice was distant. I turned back.

"Yes, I'm here, J! I'm here! It's gonna be alright."

"The hippo, Mo..."

"What?!"

"The hippo." He was muttering. "You were the hippo."

I grabbed his shoulders.

"Oh, please, J —don't speak nonsense. Not now."

His lips came together and curled at the edges. Slowly his eyelids came down.

"Oh, not now!"

I looked up.

"Someone get a doctor!"

I held his head. The blood coursed out of his ear and into my palm. His hair, on the side, was stained red.

I felt a hand on my neck. I turned. It was Vern. I put my head against his shoulder.

"How delightful is the day," he said.

He pulled away and looked at the ground. The paper was everywhere. He picked up a sheet. I looked him in the eyes. He thrust it forward.

"Here," he said. "You might as well start here."

Acknowledgments

A mentor of mine once wrote that a book is product of those who believe in it. So too this one. I'd like to thank, in addition to my parents and brother and grandfather, to whom this work is in the first place dedicated and without whose constant support and love it could never have happened, the following other people, in no particular order, but with all the love and appreciation that order generally conveys: Paul Hendrickson, for being the most honest, caring and intelligent guidance counselor/editor/friend a young, wannabe anything (but especially a writer) could have; Al Filreis, whose constant networking on my behalf, and editorial oversight additionally, helped me realize a potential sometimes only he saw; Rob Weisbach, whose editorial brilliance and friendship in the last couple of years brought this manuscript from its infancy to its current, hopefully-less-than-infantile state; David Groff and Stephanie Reents, who in their own ways, left indelible marks on the piece; Adam Goodman, Brad Rubin, Ari Barzideh, whose tolerance of my personality (especially in Europe) allowed me the hours in their presence which, in part, inspired this story; all of my friends and collaborators at Penn, especially those in the OCP, at the DP and in the English department; and finally to those of you – you know who you are – who read the piece – or simply read me – when it – or I – was most raw and who then saw inside the life of things. Let's do it again.

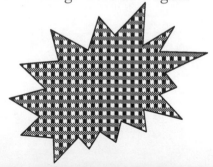